SO MUCH FOR A VACATION...

We had just reached the window when we heard the scream.

It was like no sound I had ever heard, thin and high and horribly final. The station was huge and noisy but the scream cut through the crowd like a scalpel. Everybody stopped and turned to see where it had come from. Even Tim heard it. "Oh dear," he said. "It sounds like someone has stepped on a cat."

Already a police car had arrived and several uniformed guards were hurrying toward the trains. I strained to hear what the crowd was saying. They were speaking French, of course. That didn't make it any easier.

"What's happened?"

"It's terrible. Somebody has fallen under a train."

"It was a steward. He was on the train from London. He fell off a platform."

"Is he hurt?"

"He's dead. Crushed by a train."

I heard all of it. I understood some of it. I didn't like any of it. A steward? Off the London train? Somehow I didn't need to ask his name.

"Tim," I asked, "what's the French for murder?"

Tim shrugged. "Why do you want to know?"

"I don't know." I stepped onto the escalator and allowed it to carry me down. "I've just got a feeling it's something we're going to need."

THREE OF DIAMONDS

Three Diamond Brothers Mysteries

BOOKS BY ANTHONY HOROWITZ

The Devil and His Boy

THE ALEX RIDER ADVENTURES
Stormbreaker
Point Blank
Skeleton Key
Eagle Strike
Scorpia
Ark Angel

THE DIAMOND BROTHERS MYSTERIES
Public Enemy Number Two
The Falcon's Malteser
Three of Diamonds
South By Southeast

THREE OF DIAMONDS

Three Diamond Brothers Mysteries

ANTHONY HOROWITZ

PUFFIN BOOKS

PUFFIN BOOKS
Published by the Penguin Group
Penguin Young Readers Group, 345 Hudson Street, New York, New York 10014, U.S.A.
Penguin Group (Canada), 90 Eglinton Avenue East, Suite 700,
Toronto, Ontario, Canada M4P 2Y3 (a division of Pearson Penguin Canada Inc.)
Penguin Books Ltd, 80 Strand, London WC2R 0RL, England
Penguin Ireland, 25 St Stephen's Green, Dublin 2, Ireland (a division of Penguin Books Ltd)
Penguin Group (Australia), 250 Camberwell Road, Camberwell, Victoria 3124, Australia
(a division of Pearson Australia Group Pty Ltd)
Penguin Books India Pvt Ltd, 11 Community Centre, Panchsheel Park,
New Delhi - 110 017, India
Penguin Group (NZ), Cnr Airborne and Rosedale Roads, Albany, Auckland,
New Zealand (a division of Pearson New Zealand Ltd)
Penguin Books (South Africa) (Pty) Ltd, 24 Sturdee Avenue, Rosebank,
Johannesburg 2196, South Africa

Registered Offices: Penguin Books Ltd, 80 Strand, London WC2R 0RL, England

The Blurred Man first published in Great Britain by Walker Books Ltd, 2002
The French Confection first published in Great Britain by Walker Books Ltd, 2002
I Know What You Did Last Wednesday first published in Great Britain by
Walker Books Ltd, 2002
Published simultaneously in the United States of America by Philomel Books and
Puffin Books, divisions of Penguin Young Readers Group, 2005

9 10

The Blurred Man copyright © Anthony Horowitz, 2002
The French Confection copyright © Anthony Horowitz, 2002
I Know What You Did Last Wednesday copyright © Anthony Horowitz, 2002

LIBRARY OF CONGRESS CATALOGING-IN-PUBLICATION DATA
Horowitz, Anthony, 1955–
Three of diamonds : a Diamond Brothers mystery / Anthony Horowitz.
p. cm.
Summary: A collection of three Diamond Brothers mysteries in which Tim and Nick
bungle their way through a search for a missing philanthropist, find themselves in a
Parisian prison, and are stranded on a Scottish island with a murderer.
Content: The blurred man — The French confection — I know what you did last Wednesday.

Puffin Books ISBN 978-0-14-240298-6

[1. Brothers—Fiction. 2. London (England)—Fiction. 3.England—Fiction.
4. Paris (France)—Fiction. 5. France—Fiction. 6. Humorous stories. 7. Mystery and
detective stories.] I. Title: Blurred Man. II. Title: French confection.
III. Title: I know what you did last Wednesday. IV. Title.
PZ7.H7875 Th 2005 [Fic]—dc22 2004065493

Printed in the United States of America

CONTENTS

CONTENTS

THE BLURRED MAN

CONTENTS

CONTENTS

THE PEN PAL

I knew the American was going to mean trouble, the moment he walked through the door. He only made it on the third attempt. It was eleven o'clock in the morning but clearly he'd been drinking since breakfast—and breakfast had probably come out of a bottle, too. The smell of whiskey was so strong it made my eyes water. Drunk at eleven o'clock! I didn't like to think what it was doing to him, but if I'd been his liver I'd have been applying for a transplant.

He managed to find a seat and slumped into it. The funny thing was, he was quite smartly dressed: a suit and a tie that looked expensive. I got the feeling straightaway that this was someone with money. He was wearing gold-rimmed glasses, and as far as I could tell we were talking real gold. He was about forty years old, with hair that was just turning gray and eyes that were just turning yellow. That must have been the whiskey. He took out a cigarette and lit it. Blue smoke filled the room. This man would not have been a good advertisement for the National Health Service.

"My name is Carter," he said at last. He spoke with an American accent. "Joe Carter. I just got in from Chicago. And I've got a problem."

"I can see that," I muttered.

He glanced at me with one eye. The other eye looked somewhere over my shoulder. "Who are you?" he demanded.

"I'm Nick Diamond."

"I don't need a smart-aleck kid. I'm looking for a private detective."

"That's him over there," I said, indicating the desk and my big brother, Tim.

"You want a coffee, Mr. Carver?" Tim asked.

"It's not Carver. It's Carter. With a *t*," the American growled.

"I'm out of tea. How about a hot chocolate?"

"I don't want a hot anything!" Carter sucked on the cigarette. "I want help. I want to hire you. What do you charge?"

Tim stared. Although it was hard to believe, the American was offering him money. This was something that didn't happen often. Tim hadn't really made any money since he'd worked as a policeman, and even then the police dogs had earned more than him. At least they'd bitten the right man. As a private detective, Tim had been a total calamity. I'd helped him solve one or two cases, but most of the time I was stuck at school. Right now it was the week of vacation—six weeks before Christmas, and once again it didn't look like our stockings were going to be full. Unless you're talking holes. Tim had just seven cents left in his bank account. We'd written a begging letter to our mom and dad in Australia but were still saving up for the stamp.

I coughed and Tim jerked upright in his chair, trying to

look businesslike. "You need a private detective?" he said. "Fine. That's me. But it'll cost you fifty a day, plus expenses."

"You take traveler's checks?"

"That depends on the traveler."

"I don't have cash."

"Traveler's checks are fine," I said.

Joe Carter pulled out a bundle of blue traveler's checks, then fumbled for a pen. For a moment I was worried that he'd be too drunk to sign them. But somehow he managed to scribble his name five times on the dotted lines, and slid the checks across. "All right," he said. "That's five hundred dollars."

"Five hundred dollars!" Tom squeaked. The last time he'd had that much money in his hand he'd been playing Monopoly. "Five hundred dollars...?"

Carter nodded. "Right. So now let me tell you where I'm coming from."

"I thought you were coming from Chicago," Tim said.

"I mean, let me tell you my problem. I got into England last Tuesday, a little less than a week ago. I'm staying in a hotel in the West End. The Ritz."

"You'd be crackers to stay anywhere else," Tim said.

"Yeah." Carter stubbed his cigarette out in the ashtray. Except we didn't have an ashtray. The smell of burning wood rose from the surface of Tim's desk. "I'm a writer, Mr. Diamond. You may have read some of my books."

That was unlikely—unless he wrote children's books.

Tim had recently started *Lemony Snickett* for the fourth time.

"I'm pretty well known in the States," Carter continued. *"The Big Bullet. Death in the Afternoon. Rivers of Blood.* Those are some of my titles."

"Romances?" Tim asked.

"No. They're crime novels. I'm successful. I make a ton of money out of my writing—but, you know, I believe in sharing it around. I'm not married. I don't have kids. So I give it to charity. All sorts of charities. Mostly back home in the States, of course, but also in other parts of the world."

I wondered if he'd like to make a donation to the bankrupt brothers of dumb detectives, a little charity of my own. But I didn't say anything.

"Now, a couple of years back I heard of a charity operating here in England," he went on. "It was called Dream Time and I kind of liked the sound of it. Dream Time was there to help kids get more out of life. It bought computers and books and special equipment for schools. It also bought schools. It helped train kids who wanted to get into sports. Or who wanted to paint. Or who had never traveled." Carter glanced at me. "How old are you, son?" he asked.

"Thirteen," I said.

"I bet you make wishes sometimes."

"Yes. But unfortunately Tim is still here."

"Dream Time would help you. They make wishes come true." Carter reached into his pocket and took out a hip flask. He unscrewed it and threw it back. It seemed to do him good. "A little Scotch," he explained.

"I thought you were American," Tim said.

"I gave Dream Time two million dollars of my money because I believed in them!" Carter exclaimed. "Most of all, I believed in the man behind Dream Time. He was a saint. He was a lovely guy. His name was Lenny Smile."

I noticed that Carter was talking about Smile in the past tense. I was beginning to see the way this conversation might be going.

"What can I tell you about Lenny?" Carter went on. "Like me, he never married. He didn't have a big house or a fancy car or anything like that. In fact he lived in a small apartment in a part of London called Battersea. Dream Time had been his idea and he worked for it seven days a week, three hundred and sixty-five days a year. Lenny loved leap years because then he could work three hundred and sixty-six days a year. That was the sort of man he was. When I heard about him, I knew I had to support his work. So I gave him a quarter of a million dollars. And then another quarter. And so on..."

"So what's the problem, Mr. Starter?" Tim asked. "You want your money back?"

"Hell, no! Let me explain. I loved this guy Lenny. I felt like I'd known him all my life. But recently, I decided we ought to meet."

"You'd never met him?"

"No. We were pen pals. We exchanged letters. Lots of

letters—and e-mails. He used to write to me and I'd write back. That's how I got to know him. But I was busy with my work. And he was busy with his. We never met. We never even spoke. And then, recently, I suddenly realized I needed a break. I'd been working so hard, I decided to come over to England and have a vacation.

"I wrote to Lenny and told him I'd like to meet him. He was really pleased to hear from me. He said he wanted to show me all the work he'd been doing. All the children who'd benefited from the money I'd sent. I was really looking forward to the trip. He was going to meet me at Heathrow Airport."

"How would you know what he looked like if you'd never met?" I asked.

Carter blushed. "Well, I did sometimes wonder about that. So once I'd arranged to come I asked him to send me a photograph of himself."

He reached into his jacket and took out a photograph. He handed it to me.

The picture showed a man standing in front of a café in what could have been London or Paris. It was hard to be sure. I could see the words CAFÉ DEBUSSY written on the windows. But the man himself was harder to make out. Whoever had taken the photograph should have asked Dream Time for a new camera. It was completely out of focus. I could just make out a man in a black suit with a full-length coat. He was wearing gloves and a hat. But his face was a blur. He might have had dark hair. I think he was smiling. There was a cat sitting on the pavement between his legs, and the cat was easier to make out than he was.

"It's not a very good picture," I said.

"I know." Carter took it back. "Lenny was a very shy person. He didn't even sign his letters. That's how shy he was. He told me that he didn't like going out very much. You see, there's something else you need to know about him. He was sick. He had this illness . . . some kind of allergy."

"Was Algy his doctor?" Tim asked.

"No, no. An allergy. It meant he reacted to things. Peanuts, for example. They made him swell up. And he hated publicity. There have been a couple of stories about him in the newspapers, but he wouldn't give interviews and there were never any photographs. The Queen wanted to knight him, apparently, but sadly he was also allergic to queens. All that mattered to him was his work . . . Dream Time . . . helping kids. Anyway, meeting him was going to be the biggest moment of my life . . . I was as excited as a schoolboy."

As excited as a schoolboy? Obviously Carter had never visited my school.

"Only when I got to Heathrow, Lenny wasn't there. He wasn't in London either. I never got to meet him. And you know why?"

I knew why. But I waited for Lenny to tell us.

"Lenny was buried the day before I arrived," Carter said.

"Buried?" Tim exclaimed. "Why?"

"Because it was his funeral, Mr. Diamond!" Carter lit another cigarette. "He was dead. And that's why I'm here. I want you to find out what happened."

"What did happen?" I asked.

"Well, like I told you, I arrived here at Heathrow last Tuesday. All I could think about was meeting Lenny Smile, shaking that man's hand and telling him just how much he meant to me. When he didn't show up, I didn't even check into my hotel. I went straight to the offices of Dream Time. And that was when they told me . . ."

"Who told you?" I asked.

"A man called Hoover. Rodney Hoover . . ."

"That name sucks," Tim said.

Carter ignored him. "He worked for Lenny, helping him run Dream Time. There's another assistant there, too, called Fiona Lee. She's very posh. Upper-class, you know? They have an office just the other side of Battersea Bridge. It's right over the café you saw in that photo. Anyway, it seems that just a few days after I e-mailed Lenny to tell him I was coming, he got killed in a horrible accident, crossing the road."

"He fell down a manhole?" Tim asked.

"No, Mr. Diamond. He got run over. Hoover and Lee actually saw it happen. If they hadn't been there, the police wouldn't even have known it was Lenny."

"Why is that?"

"Because he was run over by a steamroller." Carter shuddered. Tim shivered. Even the desk light flickered. I had to admit, it was a pretty horrible way to go. "He was flattened," the American went on. "They told me that the ambulance people had to fold him before they could get him onto a stretcher. He was buried last week. At Brompton Cemetery, near Fulham."

Brompton. That was where the master criminal known as the Falcon had been buried, too. Tim and I had gone to the cemetery at the end of our first ever case.* We were lucky we weren't still there.

"This guy Rodney Hoover tells me he's winding down Dream Time," Carter went on. "He says it wouldn't be the same without Lenny, and he doesn't have the heart to go on without him. I had a long talk with him in his office and I have to tell you . . . I didn't like it."

"You don't think it's a nice office?" Tim asked.

"I think something strange is going on."

Tim blinked. "What exactly do you think is strange?"

Carter almost choked on his cigarette. "Damnit!" he yelled. "You don't think there's anything unusual in a guy getting run over by a steamroller? It happens in the middle of the night and just a few days before he's due to have a meeting with someone who's given him two million dollars! And the next thing you hear, the charity he'd set up is suddenly shutting down! You don't think that's all a little strange?"

"It's certainly strange that it happened in the middle of

*See *The Falcon's Malteser*

the night," Tim agreed. "Why wasn't he in bed?"

"I don't know why he wasn't in bed—but I'll tell you this: I think he was murdered. A man doesn't walk in front of a steamroller. But maybe he's pushed. Maybe this has got something to do with money . . . my money. Maybe somebody didn't want us to meet! I know that if I was writing this as a novel, that's the way it would turn out. Anyway, there are plenty of private detectives in London. If you're not interested, I can find someone who is. So are you going to look into this for me or not?"

Tim glanced at the traveler's checks. He scooped them up. "Don't worry, Mr. Carpark," he said. "I'll find the truth. The only question is—where do I find you?"

"I'm still at the Ritz," Carter said. "Ask for Room eight."

"I'll ask for you," Tim said. "But if you're out, I suppose the roommate will have to do."

We changed the traveler's checks into cash and blew some of it on the first decent meal we'd had in a week. Tim was in a good mood. He even let me have a dessert.

"I can't believe it!" he exclaimed as the waitress served us two ice cream sundaes. The service in the restaurant was so slow that they were more like Mondays by the time they arrived. "Five hundred dollars! That's more money than I've earned in a month."

"It's more money than you've earned in a year," I reminded him.

"And all because some crazy American thinks his pen pal was murdered."

"How do you know he wasn't?"

"Intuition." Tim tapped the side of his nose. "I can't explain it to you, kid. I've just got a feeling."

"You've also got ice cream on your nose," I said.

After lunch we took the bus over to Fulham. I don't know why Tim decided to start in Brompton Cemetery. Maybe he wanted to visit it for old times' sake. It had been more than a year since we'd last been there, but the place hadn't changed. And why should it have? I doubted any of the residents had complained. None of them would have had the energy to redecorate. The gravestones were as weird as ever, some of them like Victorian telephone boxes, others like miniature castles with doors fastened by rusting chains and padlocks. You'd have needed a skeleton key to open them. The place was divided into separate areas: some old, some more modern. There must have been thousands of people there, but of course none of them offered to show us the way to Smile's grave. We had to find it on our own.

It took us about an hour. It was on the edge of the cemetery, overshadowed by the football stadium next door. We might never have found it except that the grave had been recently dug. That was one clue. And there were fresh flowers. That was another. Smile had been given a lot of flowers. In fact, if he hadn't been dead he could have opened a florist's. I read the gravestone:

LENNY SMILE

APRIL 31st 1955—NOVEMBER 11th 2001

A WONDERFUL MAN, CALLED TO REST.

We stood in silence for a moment. It seemed too bad that someone who had done so much for children all over the world hadn't even made it to fifty. I glanced at the biggest bunch of flowers on the grave. There was a card attached. It was signed in green ink, *With love, from Rodney Hoover and Fiona Lee.*

There was a movement on the other side of the cemetery. I had thought we were alone when we arrived, but now I realized that there was a man, watching us. He was a long way away, standing behind one of the taller gravestones, but even at that distance I thought there was something familiar about him, and I found myself shivering without quite knowing why. He was wearing a full-length coat with gloves and a hat. I couldn't make out his face. From this distance, it was just a blur. And that was when I realized. I knew exactly where I'd seen him before. I started forward, running toward him. At that moment he turned around and hurried off, moving away from me.

"Nick!" Tim called out.

I ignored him and ran through the cemetery. There was a gravestone in the way and I jumped over it. Maybe that wasn't a respectful thing to do but I wasn't feeling exactly religious. I reached the main path and sprinted forward. I didn't know if Tim was following me or not. I didn't care.

The northern gates of the cemetery opened onto Old Brompton Road. I burst out and stood there, catching my breath. It came as a shock, coming from the land of the dead into that of the living, with buses and cabs roaring past. An old woman, wrapped in three cardigans, was selling flowers right next to the gate. Business couldn't have been good. Half the flowers were as dead as the people they were meant for. I went over to her.

"Excuse me . . ." I said. "Did someone just come out through this gate?"

The old woman shook her head. "No, dear. I didn't see anyone."

"Are you sure? A man in a long coat. He was wearing a hat . . ."

"People don't come out of the cemetery," the old woman said. "When they get there, they stay there."

A moment later, Tim proved her wrong by appearing at the gate. "What is it, Nick?" he asked.

I looked up and down the pavement. There was nobody in sight. Had I imagined it? No. I was certain. The man I had seen in Joe Carter's photograph had been in the cemetery less than a minute ago. Once I'd spotted him, he had run away.

But that was impossible, wasn't it?

If it was Lenny Smile that I had just seen, then who was buried in the grave?

DEAD MAN'S FOOTSTEPS

We began our search for Lenny Smile the next day—at the Battersea offices of the charity he had created.

I knew the building, of course, from the photograph Carter had shown us. Dream Time's headquarters were above the Café Debussy, which was in the middle of a row of half-derelict shops a few minutes' walk from the River Thames. It was hard to believe that a charity worth millions of dollars could operate from such a small, shabby place. But maybe that was the point. Maybe they didn't want to spend the money they raised on plush offices in the West End. It's the same reason why Oxfam shops always look so run-down. That way they can afford another ox.

But the inside of Dream Time was something else. The walls had been knocked through to create an open-spaced area with carpets that reached up to your ankles and leather furniture you couldn't believe had started life as a cow. The light fixtures looked Italian. Low lighting at high prices. There were framed pictures on the walls of smiling children from around the world: Asia, Africa, Europe, and so on. The receptionist was smiling, too. We already knew that the place was being shut down, and I could see that she didn't have a lot to do. She'd just finished polishing her nails when we walked in.

While we were waiting she started polishing her teeth.

At last a door opened and Fiona Lee walked in. At least, I guessed it was her. We'd called that morning and made an appointment. She was tall and slim, with her dark hair tied back in such a vicious bun that you'd expect it to explode at any moment. She had the looks of a model, but I'm talking the kind they give away free at McDonald's. All plastic. Her makeup was perfect. Her clothes were perfect. Everything about her was perfect, down to the last detail. Either she spent hours getting ready every morning, or she slept hanging in the closet so that she didn't rumple her skin.

"Good morning," she said. Joe Carter had been right about her. She had such a posh accent that when she spoke you heard every letter. "My name is Fiona Lee."

We introduced ourselves.

She looked from Tim to me and back again. She didn't seem impressed. "Do come in," she said. She spun around on her heel. With heels like hers I was surprised she didn't drill a hole in the floor.

We followed her down a corridor lined with more smiling kids. At the end was a door that led to an office on a corner, with views of Battersea Park one way and the Thames the other. Rodney Hoover was sitting behind a desk cluttered with papers and half-dead potted plants, talking on the telephone. An ugly desk for a very ugly man. Both of them looked like they were made of wood. He was getting fat and might have been a little less fat if he'd taken up running. He had drooping shoulders and jet-black hair that oozed oil. He was wearing an old-fashioned suit that was too small for him and glasses that were too big. As he finished his call, I noticed that he had horrible teeth. In fact the last time I'd seen teeth like that, they'd been in a dog. Mrs. Lee signaled and we sat down. Hoover hung up. He had been speaking with a strong accent that could have been Russian or German. He had bad breath. No wonder the potted plants on his desk were wilting.

"Good morning," he said.

"This is Tim Diamond, Mr. Hoover," Mrs. Lee said. She pronounced his name *Teem Day-mond*. "He telephoned this morning."

"Oh yes. Yes!" Hoover turned to Tim. "I am being sorry that I cannot help you, Mr. Diamond." His English was terrible, although his breath was worse. "Right now, you see, Mrs. Lee and I are closing down Dream Time, so if you have come about your little brother . . ."

"I don't need charity," I said.

"We helped a boy like you just a month ago," Fiona Lee said. She blinked, and her eyelashes seemed to wave goodbye. "He had always wanted to climb mountains, but he was afraid of heights."

"So did you buy him a small mountain?" Tim asked.

"No. We got him help from a psychiatrist. Then we paid for him to fly to Mount Everest. That little boy went all the way to the top! And although he unfortunately fell off, he was happy. That is the point of our work, Mr. Diamond. We use the money that we raise to make children happy."

"And take the case of Billy!" Hoover added. He pointed at yet another photograph on the wall. If Dream Time had helped many more kids, they'd have run out of wall. "Billy was a boy who wanted to be a dancer. He was being bullied at school. So we hired some bullies to bully the bullies for Billy and now, you see, Billy is in the ballet!"

"Bully for Billy," I muttered.

"So how can we be of helping to you, Mr. Diamond?" Hoover asked.

"I have some questions," Tim said, "about a friend of yours called Lenny Smile."

Both Rodney Hoover and Fiona Lee froze. Hoover licked his teeth, which couldn't have been a lot of fun. Fiona had gone pale. Even her makeup seemed to have lost some of its color. "Why are you asking questions about Lenny?" she asked.

"Because that way people give me answers," Tim replied. "It's what I do. I'm a private detective."

There was an ugly silence. I had to say that it suited Rodney Hoover.

"Lenny is dead," he said. "You know very well that he's lying there in Brompton Cemetery. Yes? What could you possibly want to know about him?"

"I know he's dead," Tim said. "But I'd be interested to know exactly how he died. I understand you were there."

"We were there," Fiona said. A single tear had appeared

in the corner of her eye and began to trickle down her cheek. "Poor, poor Lenny! It was the most ghastly, horrible moment in my life, Mr. Diamond."

"I don't suppose it was a terrific moment for him either," I muttered.

She ignored me. "It was about eleven o'clock. Mr. Hoover and I had gone to see him. He didn't like to come out of his apartment, so we often went over there to tell him how much money we had raised and how the charity was progressing. We talked. We had a glass of wine. And then we left."

"Lenny said he would come down with us to the car," Hoover continued. "It was a very beautiful night. He wanted to have some of the fresh air . . . you know? And so, we left the apartment together."

"Lenny was a little bit ahead of us," Fiona Lee explained. "He was a fast walker. Mr. Hoover stopped to tie his shoelaces and I waited for him. Lenny stepped into the road. And then . . ."

"The steamroller was going too fast." He swore quietly in a foreign language. Fiona sighed. "But the driver was on his way home. He was in a hurry. And he ran over Lenny!" He shook his head. "There was nothing, nothing we could do!"

"Do you know the driver's name?" Tim asked.

"I believe it is Krishner. Barry Krishner."

"Do you know what happened to him?"

"He is in a hospital for the hopelessly insane in North

London . . . in Harrow," Fiona said. "You can imagine that it was a dreadful experience for him, running over a man with a steamroller. But it was his fault! And because he was speeding, he killed one of the most wonderful men who ever lived. Lenny Smile! I had worked for him for twenty years. Mr. Hoover, too."

"You'd only worked for him for two years?" Tim asked.

"No. I worked with him *also* for twenty years," Hoover said. "But are you telling me, please, Mr. Diamond. Who hired you to ask these questions about Lenny Smile?"

"I never reveal the names of my clients," Tim replied. "Joe Carter wants to remain anonymous."

"Carter!" Hoover muttered. He gave Tim an ugly look. It wasn't difficult. "I could have guessed this. Yes! He came here, asking all his questions as if Fiona and me . . ." He stopped himself. "There was not one thing suspicious about his death, Mr. Diamond. It was an accident. We know. Why? Because we were there! You think someone killed him? Poppycock! Who would wish to kill him?"

"Maybe he had enemies," Tim said.

"Everybody loved Lenny," Fiona retorted. "Even his enemies loved him. All he did his whole life was give away money and help young people. That man built so many orphanages, we had to advertise for orphans to fill them."

"What else can you tell us about him?" I asked.

"It's hard to describe Lenny to someone who never met him."

"Try. Where did he live?"

"He rented an apartment on Welles Road. Number seventeen. He didn't buy anywhere because he hated spending money on himself." She took out a tiny handkerchief and dabbed the corner of her eye. "It is true that he liked to be on his own a lot."

"Why?"

"Because of his allergies."

I remembered now. Carter had said he was sick.

"What was he allergic to?" I asked.

"Many, many things," Hoover replied. "Chocolate, peanuts, yogurt, animals, rubber bands, insects . . ."

"If he was stung by a wasp, he would be in the hospital for a week," Fiona agreed.

"He was also allergic to hospitals. He had to go to a private clinic." Hoover stood up. Suddenly the interview was over. "Lenny Smile was a very unique man. He was— as you say—one in a million. And you have no right . . . no right to come here like this. You are wrong! Wrong with all your suspiciousness."

"Yes." Fiona nodded in agreement. "His death was a terrible accident. But the police investigated. They found nothing. Mr. Hoover and I were there and we saw nothing."

"You can say to your 'anonymous' client, Mr. Carter, that he should go back to Chicago," Hoover concluded. "And now, please, I think you should leave."

We left. The last thing I saw was Rodney Hoover standing

next to Fiona Lee. The two of them were holding hands. Were they just coworkers, friends . . . or something more? And there was something else. Hoover had said something. I wasn't sure what it was, but I was certain he had told me something that in fact he didn't want me to know. I tried to play back the conversation but it wouldn't come.

Tim and I left the offices of Dream Time together. Rodney Hoover and Fiona Lee had given us both the creeps. Neither of us said anything. But we both looked very carefully before we crossed the road.

At least Fiona had given us Smile's address, and as it wasn't far away, that was where we went next.

Welles Road was around the back of Battersea, not far from the famous dogs' home. The tall, redbrick buildings were all mansion apartments . . . not as big as mansions, but certainly nicer than your average apartment. There were a dozen people living in each building, with their names listed on the front door. It turned out that Smile had lived at 17A—on the fifth floor. We rang the bell, but there was no answer, so we tried 17B. There was a pause, then a woman's voice crackled over the intercom.

"Who is it?"

"We're friends of Lenny Smile," I shouted back before Tim could come up with a story of his own.

"The fifth floor!" the voice called out. There was a buzz and the door opened.

With its faded wallpaper and worn carpets, the building seemed somehow tired inside. And so were we by the time we got to the fifth floor. The elevator wasn't working. The whole place smelled damp and like yesterday's cooking. I thought you needed to be rich to live in Battersea (unless, of course, you happened to be a dog). But anyone could have lived here if they weren't fussy. The fifth floor was also the top floor. The door of 17B was open when we arrived.

"Mr. Smile is dead!"

The woman who had broken the news to us so discreetly was about eighty, with white hair that might have been a wig and a face that had long ago given up trying to look human. Her eyes, nose, and mouth all seemed to have run into one another like a melting candle. Her voice was still crackling, even without the intercom system. She was dressed in a pale orange dress decorated with flowers; the sort of material that would have looked better on a chair. There were fluffy pink slippers on her feet. Her legs—what I could see of them—were stout and hairy and made me glad that I couldn't see more.

"Who are you?" Tim asked.

"My name's Lovely."

"I'm sure it is," Tim agreed. "But what is it?"

"I just told you, dear. Lovely! Rita Lovely! I live next door to Mr. Smile. Or at least . . . I used to."

"Have you moved?" Tim asked.

Mrs. Lovely blinked at him. "No. Don't be stupid! Mr.

Smile is the one who's moved. All the way to Brompton
Cemetery!"

"We know that," Tim said. "We've already been there."

"Then what do you want?"

"We want to get into his apartment."

"Why?"

I decided it was time to take over. "Mr. Smile was my
hero," I lied. I'd put on the little-boy-lost look that usually
worked with very old women. And also, for that matter, with
Tim. "He helped me."

"He gave you money?" She looked at me suspiciously.

"He saved my life. I had a rare disease."

"What disease?"

"It was so rare, it didn't have a name. Mr. Smile paid for
my medicine. I never got a chance to thank him. And I
thought, if I could at least see where he lived . . ."

That softened her. "I've got a key," she said, taking it
out of her pocket. "I was his neighbor for seven years and
I used to look after the place for him when he was away.
You seem like a nice boy, so I'll let you in, just for a few
minutes. This way . . ."

It seemed to take her forever to reach the door, but then,
she was very old. At last we were in. Mrs. Lovely closed the
door behind us and sat down to have a rest.

Smile's apartment was small and ordinary. There was a
living room, but it was so neat and impersonal that it was
hard to believe anyone had done any living there at all. There

was a three-piece sofa set, a coffee table, a few ornaments. The pictures on the wall were even less interesting than the walls they hung on. It was the same story in the other rooms. The apartment told us nothing about the person who had lived there. Even the fridge was empty.

"How often did you see Mr. Smile?" I asked.

"I never saw him," Tim replied.

"I know, Tim. I'm asking Mrs. Lovely."

"I hardly ever saw him," Mrs. Lovely said. "He kept himself to himself, if you want the truth. Although I was here the night that he got run over."

"Did you see what happened?"

"Not really, no." She shook her head vigorously and then readjusted her hair and teeth. "But I did see him go out. There were two people with him, talking to him. They seemed to be helping him down the stairs."

"Helping him?"

"One on each side of him. A man and a woman . . ."

That would have been Rodney Hoover and Fiona Lee.

"After they'd gone, I heard the most terrible noise. It was a sort of rumble and then a scrunching. At first I thought it was my indigestion, but then I looked out of the window. And there they were! The two of them and the driver—"

"Barry Krishner . . ."

"I don't know his name, young man. But yes, the driver of the steamroller was there. He was looking as sick as a parrot. Hardly surprising!"

"What happened to the parrot?" Tim asked.

"There was no parrot!"

"You mean . . . it got so sick it died?"

"There was the driver, the two people I had seen on the stairs, and blood all over the road!" Mrs. Lovely sighed. "It was the worst thing I have ever seen, and I've lived through two world wars! Blood everywhere! Lots and lots and lots of blood—"

"Thank you," Tim interrupted, going pale.

"Were there no other witnesses?" I asked.

"Just one." Mrs. Lovely leaned forward. "There was a balloon seller on the other side of the road. He must have seen everything. I've already been asked about him once, so before you ask me again, let me tell you that I don't know his name or where he had come from. He was an old man. He had a beard and about fifty helium balloons. Floating above his head."

"Why was his beard floating over his head?" Tim asked.

"The balloons, Tim!" I growled. I turned to Mrs. Lovely. "Is there anything else you can tell us?" I asked. "Anything about Lenny Smile?"

"No. Not really." Suddenly there were tears in the old woman's eyes. She took out a handkerchief and blew her nose loudly. "I will miss him. It's true I hardly ever saw him, but he was a gentleman. Look at this note he sent me. It was my ninety-first birthday last week and he slipped it under the door."

She produced a crumpled sheet of paper, torn out of a notebook. There were a couple of lines written in green ink:

Dear Mrs. Lovely,
I hope you have a lovely birthday.
L.S.

That was all. The note couldn't have been less interesting or informative. And yet, even so, I thought there was something strange about it, something that didn't quite add up. I handed it back.

"Nobody else remembered my birthday." Mrs. Lovely sighed. "I didn't get any cards. But then, most of my friends were blown up in the war . . ." She wiped her eyes. "I couldn't have asked for a more quiet neighbor," she said. "And now that he's gone, I'll really miss him."

How could she miss him when she had hardly ever met him? And why had Lenny Smile taken so much care not to be seen? I was beginning to realize that it wasn't just Carter's photograph that had been blurred. The same thing could be said for everything in Lenny Smile's life.

We found Barry Krishner, the steamroller driver, easily enough. There was only one institute for the hopelessly insane in Harrow. Well, two if you count the famous private school that was just a little farther down the road. The hospital was a big, Victorian building, set in its own grounds with a path leading up to the front door.

"Are you sure this is the right place?" Tim asked.

"Yes," I said. "They've even got crazy paving."

I have to say, I was a bit worried about going into a mental asylum with Tim. I wondered if they'd let him out again. But it was too late to back out now. One of the doctors, a man called Eams, was waiting for us at the entrance. He was a short man, bald with a little beard that could have been bought at a joke shop. We introduced ourselves and he led us out of the winter sunlight into the gloomy heart of the building.

"Krishner has responded very well to treatment," he said. "Otherwise I would not let you speak with him. Even so, I must ask you to be extremely careful. As I am sure you can imagine, running someone over with a steamroller is a very upsetting experience."

"For Lenny Smile?" Tim asked.

"For the driver! When Krishner first came here, he was in a state of shock. He ate very little. He barely spoke. Every night he woke up screaming."

"Bad dreams, Dr. Eams?" Tim asked.

"Yes. But we have given him a lot of therapy and there has been considerable improvement. However, please, Mr. Diamond, try not to refer to what happened. Don't mention any of the details—the steamroller, the accident itself. You have to be discreet!"

"Discreet is my middle name!" Tim nodded.

"And also please bear in mind, he is not a lunatic. He is here as my patient. So don't say anything that would make him think he is mentally ill."

Tim laughed. "I'd be mad to do that!" He nudged the doctor. "So, where's his padded cell?"

Barry Krishner was sitting in a small, old-fashioned room that could just as easily have belonged to a seaside hotel as an asylum. A large window looked out onto the garden and there were no bars. He was a small, gray-haired man, dressed in an old sports jacket and dark pants. I noticed his eyes blinked a lot behind his glasses, and he kept picking his nails. Otherwise it would have been impossible to tell that he had, until recently, been in shock.

"Good afternoon, Barry," Dr. Eams said. "These people want to ask you some very important questions about Lenny Smile." Krishner twitched as if he had just been electrocuted. Dr. Eams smiled and continued in a soothing tone of voice. "You have nothing to worry about. They're not going to upset you." He nodded at Tim.

"I guess you must be feeling a bit flat," Tim began.

Krishner whimpered and twisted in his chair. Dr. Eams frowned at Tim, then gently took hold of Krishner's arm. "Are you all right, Barry?" he asked. "Would you like me to get you a drink?"

"Good idea," Tim agreed. "How about a Coke with crushed ice?"

Krishner shrieked. His glasses had slipped off his nose and one of his eyes had gone bloodshot.

"Mr. Diamond!" Eams was angry now. "Please could you be careful what you say. You told me you were going to ask Barry what he saw outside Lenny Smile's house."

"You're absolutely right, Doc." Tim winked. "I think it's time we got to the crunch . . ."

Krishner went completely white. I thought he was going to pass out.

Dr. Eams stared at Tim. "For heaven's sake . . . !" he rasped.

"Can we run over a couple things?" Tim asked.

Krishner began to foam at the mouth.

"You see, I really want to crack this case. Although I have to say, clues are a bit thin on the ground . . ."

Barry Krishner screamed and jumped out of the window. Without opening it. Alarms went off all over the hospital and, two minutes later, Tim and I were being escorted off the premises with the gates locked securely behind us.

"They weren't very helpful," Tim muttered. "Do you think it was something I said?"

I didn't answer. We had spent the whole day following in a supposedly dead man's footsteps. They had led us nowhere.

So where did we go now?

A NIGHT AT THE CIRCUS

The next day was a Saturday. Tim was in a bad mood when he came in for breakfast. He'd obviously gotten up on the wrong side of the bed: not a good idea, since he slept next to the window. At least there was food in the fridge. The money that Joe Carter had paid us would last us a month, and that morning I'd cooked up eggs, bacon, tomatoes, sausages, and beans. The papers had arrived—the *Sun* for me, the *Dandy* for Tim. An hour later the two of us were so full we could barely move. There's nothing like a great British breakfast for a great British heart attack.

But the truth is, we were both down in the dumps—and this time I don't mean the apartment. We were no nearer to finding the truth about Smile. Rodney Hoover and Fiona Lee, the pair who ran Dream Time, were obviously creepy. According to Mrs. Lovely, the next-door neighbor, they had half-carried Smile downstairs just before his fatal accident. Had he been drunk? Or drugged? They could have thrown him in front of the steamroller—but if so, why? As Tim would undoubtedly have said, they'd have needed a pressing reason.

Barry Krishner, the driver of the steamroller, hadn't been able to tell us anything. After his encounter with Tim, it would probably be years before he talked again. He might babble and gibber, but I guessed talking would be a little beyond him. The police had presumably investigated and found nothing. Maybe there was nothing to find.

And yet . . .

Part of me still wondered if Lenny Smile really was dead. I remembered the man I had glimpsed in Brompton Cemetery. He had looked remarkably like the man I had seen in the photograph, and had certainly taken off fast enough when I spotted him. But if Lenny wasn't dead, where was he? And who was it who had disappeared under the steamroller?

"I give up!" Tim exclaimed.

He seemed to be reading my mind. "This isn't an easy case," I agreed.

"No!" He pointed. "I'm talking about this crossword in the *Dandy*!"

I ignored him and flicked over the page in my newspaper. And that was when I saw it. It was on the same page as the horoscopes. An advertisement for a circus in Battersea Park.

Direct from Moscow
THE RUSSIAN STATE CIRCUS
Starring
The Flying Karamazov Brothers
Karl "On Your" Marx—The Human Cannonball
The Fabulous Tina Trotsky
Three Sisters on Unicycles
And much, much more!

There was a picture showing a big top, but it was what was in front that had caught my eye. It was a figure in silhouette. A man selling balloons.

"Look at this, Tim!" I exclaimed, sliding the newspaper toward him.

Tim quickly read the page. "That's amazing!" he said. "I'm going to meet an old friend!"

"What are you talking about?"

"My horoscope. That's what it says . . ."

"Not the horoscopes, Tim! Look at the advertisement underneath!"

Tim read it. "This is no time to be going to the circus, Nick," he said. "We're on a case!"

"But look at the balloon seller!" I took a deep breath. "Don't you remember what Mrs. Lovely said? There was a witness when Lenny Smile was killed. It was a man selling balloons. I thought that was odd at the time. Why should there have been a balloon seller in Battersea Park in the middle of the night?"

"He could have been lost . . ."

"I don't think so. I think he must have been part of the circus. There's a picture of him here in the paper. Maybe the balloon seller was advertising the circus!"

"You mean . . . on his balloons?"

"Brilliant, Tim! Got it in one."

Tim ripped the page of the newspaper in half. He must have accidentally caught hold of the tablecloth, because he ripped that in half, too. He folded the paper into his top pocket. "It's your turn to do the dishes," he said. "Then let's go!"

In fact we didn't go back to Battersea until that evening. According to the advertisement, there was only one perform- ance of the circus that day—at seven-thirty—and I didn't see any point in showing up before. If the balloon seller really was part of the big top, he'd probably be somewhere around during the performance. We would catch up with him then.

I don't know what you think about circuses. To be honest, I've never been a big fan. When you really think about it, is there anybody in the world less funny than a clown? And what can you say about somebody who has spent half their life learning how to balance thirty spinning plates and an umbrella on their nose? Okay. It's clever. But there simply have to be more useful things to do with your time! And, for that matter, with your nose. There was a time when they used to have animals—lions and elephants—performing in the ring. They were banned and I have to agree that was a good idea. But for my money they could ban the rest of the per- formers too, and put everyone out of their misery. I'm sorry. I've heard of people who have run away to join a circus, but speaking personally I'd run away to avoid seeing one.

But that said, I had to admit that the Russian State Circus looked interesting. It had parked its tent right in the middle of the park and there was something crazy and old-

fashioned about the bright colors and the fluttering flags all
edged silver by a perfect November moon. Four or five
hundred people had turned out to see the show, and there
were stilt-walkers and jugglers keeping the people amused as
they lined up to get in. As well as the tent itself there were
about a dozen trailers parked on the grass, forming a miniature town. Some of these were modern and ugly. But there
were also wooden trailers, painted red, blue, and gold, that
made me think of Russian gypsies and Russian palm-
readers—old crones telling your future by candlelight. Tim
had had his palm read once, when we were in Torquay. The
palm-reader had laughed so much she'd had to lie down . . .
and that was only the contents of one finger on his left hand.

We bought tickets for the show. Tim wanted to see it,
and having come all this way across London, I thought why
not? We bought two of the last seats and followed the crowd
in. Somehow the tent seemed even bigger inside than out. It
was lit by flaming torches on striped, wooden poles. Gray
smoke coiled in the air and dark shadows flickered across
the ring. The whole place was bathed in a strange, red glow
that seemed to transport us back to another century. The
top of the tent was a tangle of ropes and wires, of rings and
trapezes, all promises of things to come, but right then the
ring was empty. There were wooden benches raked up in a
steep bank, seven rows deep, forming a circle all around the
sawdust. We were in the cheapest seats, one row from the
back. As a treat, I'd bought Tim a stick of cotton candy. By

the time the show started, he'd managed to get it all over himself as well as about half a dozen people on either side.

A band took its place on the far side of the ring. There were five players, dressed in old, shabby tailcoats. They had faces to match. The conductor looked about a hundred years old. I just hoped the music wouldn't get too exciting—I doubted his heart would stand it. With a trembling hand, he raised his baton and the band began to play. Unfortunately, the players all began at different times and what followed was a tremendous wailing and screeching as they all raced to get to the end first. But the conductor didn't seem to notice and the audience loved it. They'd come out for a good time, and even when the violinist fell off his chair and the trombonist dropped his trombone, they cheered and applauded.

By now I was almost looking forward to seeing the show . . . but as things turned out, we weren't going to see anything of the performance that night.

The band came to the end of its first piece and began its second—which could have been either a new piece or the same piece played again. It was hard to be sure. I was glancing at the audience when suddenly I froze. There was a man sitting in the front row, right next to the gap in the tent where the performers would come in. He was wearing a dark coat, a hat, and gloves. He was too far away. Or maybe it was the poor light or the smoke. But once again his face was blurred. Even so, I knew him at once.

It was the man from the Brompton Cemetery.

The man in the photograph at the Café Debussy.

Lenny Smile!

I grabbed hold of Tim. "Quick!" I exclaimed.

"What is it?" Tim jerked away, propelling the rest of his cotton candy off the end of his stick and into the lap of the woman behind him.

"There!" I pointed. But even as I searched for Lenny across the crowded circus, I saw him get up and slip out into the night. By the time Tim had followed my finger to the other side of the tent, he had gone.

"Is it a clown?" Tim asked.

"No, Tim! It's the blurred man!"

"Who?"

"Never mind. We've got to go . . ."

"But the circus hasn't even begun!"

I dragged Tim to his feet and we made our way to the end of the row and out of the big top. My mind was racing. I still didn't know who the man in the dark coat really was. But if it was the same person I had seen at the cemetery, what was he doing here? Could he perhaps have followed us? No—that was impossible. I was sure he hadn't seen us across the crowded auditorium. He was here for another reason, and somehow I knew it had nothing to do with spinning plates and cream pies.

We left the tent just as the ringmaster, a tall man in a bright red jacket and black top hat, arrived to introduce the show. I heard him bark out a few words in Russian, but by then Tim and I were in the open air with the moon high above us, the park eerie and empty, and the trailers clustered together about a hundred feet away.

"What is it?" Tim demanded. He had forgotten why we had come and was disappointed to be missing the show.

Quickly I told him what I had seen. "We've got to look for him!" I said.

"But we don't know where he is!"

"That's why we've got to look for him."

There seemed to be only one place he could have gone. We went over to the trailers, suddenly aware how cold and quiet it was out here, away from the crowds. The first trailer was empty. The second contained a dwarf sipping sadly at a bottle of vodka. As we made our way over to the third, a man dressed in a fake leopard skin walked past carrying a steel barbell. Inside the tent I heard the ringmaster come to the end of a sentence and there was a round of applause. Either he had cracked a joke or the audience was just grateful he'd stopped talking. There was a drumroll. We approached the fourth trailer.

Lenny Smile—if that's who it was—had disappeared. But there was another dead man in Battersea Park that night.

I saw the balloons first and knew at once whose trailer this was. There were more than fifty of them, every color imaginable, clinging together as if they were somehow alive, and suddenly I knew what had just happened. The strange thing was that they did almost seem to be cowering in the corner. They weren't touching the ground. But the balloon seller was. He was stretched out on the carpet with something silver lying next to his outstretched hand.

"Don't touch it, Tim!" I warned.

Too late. Tim had already leaned over and picked it up.

It was a knife. The blade was about four inches long. It matched, perfectly, the four-inch-deep wound in the back of the balloon seller's head. There wasn't a lot of blood. The balloon seller had been an old man. Killing him had been like attacking a scarecrow.

And then somebody screamed.

I spun around. There was a little girl there in a gold dress with sequins. She was sitting on a bicycle that had only one wheel, pedaling back and forth to stop herself falling over. She was pointing at Tim, her finger trembling, her eyes filled with horror, and suddenly I was aware of the other performers appearing, coming out of their trailers as if this was the morning and they'd just woken up. Only it was the middle of the night and these people weren't dressed for bed! There was a clown in striped pants with a bowler hat and (inevitably) a red nose. There was a man on stilts. A fat man with a crash helmet. Two more sisters on unicycles. The strong man had come back with his steel barbell. A pair of identical twins stood like mirror images, identical expressions on their faces. And what they were all looking at was my big brother Tim, holding a knife and hovering in the doorway of a man who had just been murdered.

The little girl who had started it screamed once more and shouted something out. The strong man spoke. Then the clown. It all came out as gibberish to me but it didn't take a lot of imagination to work out what they were saying.

"Boris the balloon man has been murdered!"

"Dear old Boris! Who did it?"

"It must have been the idiotic-looking Englishman holding the knife."

I don't know at what precise moment the mood turned nasty, but suddenly I realized that these people no longer wanted to entertain us. The clown stepped forward and his face was twisted and ugly . . . as well as being painted white with green diamonds over his eyes. He asked Tim something, his voice cracking with emotion and his makeup doing much the same.

"I don't speak Russian," Tim said.

"You kill Boris!"

So the balloon man really was called Boris. The clown was speaking English with an incredibly thick accent, struggling to make himself understood.

"Me?" Tim smiled and innocently raised a hand. Unfortunately it was the hand that was still holding the knife.

"Why you kill Boris?"

"Actually, I think you mean 'why *did* you kill Boris,'" Tim corrected him. "You've forgotten the verb . . ."

"I don't think they want an English lesson, Tim," I said.

Tim ignored me. "I kill Boris, you kill Boris, he killed Boris!" he explained to the increasingly puzzled clown.

"I didn't kill Boris!" I exclaimed.

"They killed Boris!" the clown said.

"That's right!" Tim smiled encouragingly.

"No, we didn't!" I yelled.

It was too late. The circus performers were getting closer by the second. I didn't like the way they were looking at us. And there were more of them now. Four muscle-bound brothers in white leotards had stepped out of the shadows. The ringmaster was staring at us from the edge of the tent. I wondered who was entertaining the audience. The entire circus seemed to have congregated outside.

The ringmaster snapped out a brief command in Russian.

"Let's go, Tim!" I said.

Tim dropped the knife and we turned and fled just as the performers started toward us. As far as they were concerned, Tim had just murdered one of their number, and this was a case of an eye for an eye—or a knife wound for a knife wound. These were traveling performers. They had their own rules and to hell with the country in which they found themselves.

Tim and I took off across the park, trying to lose ourselves in the shadows. Not easy with a full moon. Something huge and solid sailed across the sky, then buried itself in the soft earth. The strong man had thrown his barbell in our direction. We were lucky—he was strong, but he obviously had lousy aim. The barbell would be found the next day sticking out of the grass like a bizarre, iron tree. Two feet to the right and we'd have been found underneath it.

But I quickly realized that this was only the start of our troubles. The entire circus troupe had abandoned the performance in order to come after us. Word had quickly got around. We had killed old Boris and now they were going to kill us. There was a dull *whoomph!* and a figure shot through the air. It was the man in the crash helmet. This had to be Karl "On Your" Marx, the human cannonball. They had fired him in our direction, and I just had time to glimpse his outstretched fists as he soared through the night sky before I grabbed hold of Tim and threw him onto the grass. Marx whizzed past. We had been standing in front of an oak tree and there was a dull crunch as he hit the trunk, ending up wedged in a fork in the branches.

"Do you think he's okay?" Tim asked.

"I don't think he's oak anything!" I replied. "Come on!"

We scrambled to our feet just as the clown set off across the grass, speeding toward us in a tiny, multicolored car. I looked ahead with a sinking heart. We really were in the middle of nowhere, with grass all around, the river in the far distance, and nobody else in sight. Anybody who had come to the park at that time of night would now be at the circus, watching the show.

"Run, Tim!" I gasped.

The clown was getting nearer. I could see his face, even less funny than usual, the greasepaint livid in the moonlight. In seconds he would catch up with us and run us down. But then there was an explosion. The hood of the car blew open, the wheels fell off, water jetted off the radiator, and smoke billowed out of the boot. The clown must have pressed the wrong button. Either that, or the car had done what it was designed for.

"Which way?" Tim panted.

I turned and looked back. For a brief, happy moment, I thought we had left the circus folk behind us, but then something whizzed through the darkness and slammed into the bark of another tree. It was a knife—but thrown from where? I looked up. There was a long telephone wire crossing the park, connected to a series of poles. And, impossibly, a man was standing, thirty feet above the ground, reaching for a second knife. It was a tightrope walker. He had followed us along the telephone wires and was there now, balancing effortlessly in midair. At the same time, I heard the sudden cough of an engine and saw a motorcycle lurch across the lawn. It was being driven by one of the brothers in white leotards. He had two more brothers standing on his shoulders. The fourth brother was on top of the other two brothers, holding what looked horribly like an automatic machine gun. The motorcycle rumbled toward us, moving slowly because of the weight of the passengers. But as I watched, it was overtaken by the three sisters on their unicycles. The moonlight sparkled not only on their sequins but on the huge swords that one of the other performers must have given them. All three of them were yelling in high-pitched voices, and somehow I knew that I wasn't hearing a Russian folk song. The man on stilts came striding toward us, moving like some monstrous insect, throwing impossibly long shadows across the grass. Somehow he had got ahead of us. And finally, to my astonishment, there was a sudden bellow and a full-sized adult elephant came lumbering out of the trees with a girl in white feathers sitting astride its neck. This would have to be the lovely Tina Trotsky. And despite the law, the Russian State Circus did have an animal or two hidden in its big top.

They had an elephant! Did they also, I wondered, have lions?

Tim had seen it, too. "They've got an elephant!" he exclaimed.

"I've seen it, Tim!"

"Is it African or Indian?"

"What?"

"I can never remember which is which!"

"What does it matter?" I almost screamed the words. "It won't make any difference when it stomps on us!"

The circus performers were closing in on us from all sides. There was a rattle from the machine gun and bullets tore into the ground, ripping up the grass. The dwarf I had seen in the trailer had woken up. It turned out he was a fire-eating dwarf . . . at least, that might explain the flame-thrower he had strapped to his back. We had the elephant, the motorcycle, and the unicycles on one side. The dwarf and the stilt man were on the other. The tightrope walker was still somewhere overhead. The human cannonball was disentangling himself from the tree.

Things weren't looking good.

But then a car suddenly appeared, speeding across the grass. It raced past one of the unicyclists, knocking her out of the way, then curved around, snapping the stilt man's stilts in half. The stilt man yelled and dove headfirst into a bank of prickers. The elephant fell back, rearing up. Tina Trotsky somersaulted backward, feathers fluttering all around her. The car skidded to a halt next to us and a door swung open.

"Get in!" someone said, and already I recognized the voice.

"Are you a taxi?" Tim asked. I think he was worrying about the fare.

"It doesn't matter what it is, Tim," I said. "Just get in!"

I pushed Tim ahead of me and dove onto the backseat. There was another rattle of machine-gun fire, a burst of flame, and a loud thud as a second knife slammed into the side of the door. But then the car was moving, bouncing up and down along the grass. I saw a bush blocking the way, right in front of us. The driver went straight through it. There was a road on the other side. A van swerved to avoid us as our tires hit concrete, and a bus swerved to avoid the van. I heard the screech of tires and the even louder screech of the drivers. There was the sound of crumpling metal. A horn blared.

But then we were away, leaving Battersea Park far behind us.

It's like I said. I'd never liked the circus. And the events of the night had done nothing to change my mind.

THE REAL LENNY SMILE

"Well, well, well. This is a very nasty surprise. The Diamond brothers! Having a night at the circus?"

It was the driver of the car, the man who had saved us, who was speaking. He had driven us directly to his office at New Scotland Yard. It had been a while since we had last seen Detective Chief Inspector Snape. But here he was, as large as life and much less enjoyable.

It had been Snape who had once employed Tim as a police officer. He had been no more than an inspector then—and he'd probably had far fewer gray hairs. He was a big, solid man who obviously worked out in a gym. Nobody was born with muscles like his. He had small blue eyes and skin the color of raw ham. He was wearing a tailor-made suit but unfortunately it had been tailor-made to somebody else. It looked as if it was about to burst. His tie was crooked. So were his teeth. So were most of the people he met.

I had never known his name was Freddy but that was what was written on the door. He had an office on the fourth floor. I had been involved with Snape twice before: once when we were on the trail of the Falcon, and once when he had forced me to share a cell with the master criminal Johnny Powers.* He wasn't someone I'd been looking

*See *Public Enemy Number Two*

forward to meeting a third time—even if he had just rescued us from the murderous crowd at the Russian State Circus.

His assistant was with him. Detective Superintendent Boyle hadn't changed much since the last time I'd seen him either. *His* first name must have been "Push." That was what was written on his door. Short and fat with curly black hair, he'd have done well in one of those TV documentaries about Neanderthal man. He was wearing a black leather jacket and faded jeans. As usual he had a couple of medallions buried in the forest of hair that sprouted up his chest and out of his open-necked shirt. Boyle looked more criminal than a criminal. He wasn't someone you'd want to meet on a dark night. He wasn't someone you'd want to meet at all.

"This is incredible!" Tim exclaimed. He turned to me. "You remember the horoscope in the newspaper! It said I was going to meet an old friend!"

"I'm not an old friend!" Snape exploded. "I hate you!"

"I'd like to get friendly with him," Boyle muttered. He took out a set of brass knuckles and slid it over his right fist. "Why don't you let the two of us go somewhere quiet, Chief . . .?"

"Forget it, Boyle!" Snape snapped. "And where did you get the brass knuckles? Have you been in the evidence room again?"

"It's mine!" Boyle protested.

"Well, put it away . . ."

Boyle slid the contraption off his hand and sulked.

Snape sat down behind his desk. Tim and I were sitting opposite him. We'd been waiting for him in the office for a couple of hours but he hadn't offered either of us so much as a cup of tea.

"What I want to know," he began, "is what the two of you were doing at the circus tonight. Why were the performers trying to kill you? And what happened to Boris the balloon seller?"

"Someone killed him," I said.

"I know that, laddy. I've seen the body. Someone stuck a knife in him."

"Yeah." I nodded. "The circus people thought it was us."

"That's an easy enough mistake to make when you two are involved." Snape smiled mirthlessly. "We went to the circus because we wanted to talk to the balloon seller," he explained. "Luckily for you. But why were you interested in him? That's what I want to know."

"I wanted to buy a balloon," I said.

"Don't lie to me, Diamond! Not unless you want to spend a few minutes on your own with Boyle."

"Just one minute," Boyle pleaded. "Thirty seconds!"

"All right," I said. "We were interested in Lenny Smile."

"Ah!" Snape's eyes widened. Boyle looked disappointed. "Why?"

"We're working for a man called Joe Carter. He's American . . ."

"He thinks Lenny Smile was murdered," Tim said.

Snape nodded. "Of course Smile was murdered," he said. "And it was the best thing that ever happened to him. If I wasn't a policeman, I'd have been tempted to murder him myself."

Tim stared. "But he was a saint!" he burbled.

"He was a crook! Lenny Smile was the biggest crook in London! Boyle and I have been investigating him for months—and we'd have arrested him if he hadn't gone under that steamroller." Snape opened a drawer and took out a file as thick as a north London telephone directory. "This is the file on Lenny Smile," he said. "Where do you want me to begin?"

"How about at the beginning?" I suggested.

"All right. Lenny Smile set up a charity called Dream Time. He employed two assistants . . . Rodney Hoover, who comes from the Ukraine. And Fiona Lee. She's from Sloane Square. We've investigated them, and as far as we can see, they're in the clear. But Smile? He was a different matter. All the money passed through his bank account. He was in financial control. And half the money that went in, never came out."

"You mean . . . he stole it?" I asked.

"Exactly. Millions of dollars that should have gone to poor children went into his own pocket. And when he did spend money on children, he got everything cheap. He provided hospitals with cheap X-ray machines that could only see halfway through. He provided schools with cheap books full of typing errrors. He took a bunch of children on a cheap adventure vacation."

"What's wrong with that?"

"It was in Afghanistan! Half the children still haven't come back! He bought headache pills that actually gave you a headache and food parcels where the parcels tasted better than the food. I'm telling you, Diamond, Lenny Smile was so crooked he makes an evening with Jack the Ripper sound like a nice idea! And I was this close to arresting him." Snape held his thumb and forefinger just an inch apart. "I already had a full-time police officer watching his apartment. It's like I say. We were just going to arrest him—but then he got killed."

"Suppose he isn't dead," I said.

Snape shook his head. "There were too many witnesses. Mrs. Lovely, the woman who lived next door, saw him leave the flat. Hoover and Lee were with him. There was Barry Krishner, the driver. And Boris . . ."

"Wait a minute!" I interrupted. "Mrs. Lovely didn't actually see anything. Barry Krishner has gone mad. I'm not sure Hoover and Lee can be trusted. And someone has just killed Boris." I remembered what Mrs. Lovely had told us. "Mrs. Lovely said that someone had been asking questions about the balloon seller," I went on. "I thought she was talking about you . . . the police! But now I wonder if it wasn't someone else. The real killer, for example!" Snape stared at me. "I think Boris saw what really happened," I concluded. "And that was why he was killed."

"Who by?" Snape demanded.

"By Lenny Smile!"

There was a long silence. Snape looked doubtful. Boyle looked . . . well, the same way Boyle always looks.

"What do you mean?" Snape demanded at length.

"It all makes sense. Lenny Smile knew that you were after him. You say you had a policeman watching his apartment?"

Snape nodded. "Henderson. He's disappeared."

"Since when?"

"He vanished a week before the accident with the steam-roller . . ."

"That was no accident!" I said. "Don't you get it, Snape? Smile knew he was cornered. You were closing in on him. And Joe Carter was coming over, too. Carter wanted to know what had happened to all the millions he'd given Dream Time. So Smile had to disappear. He faked his own death, and right now he's somewhere in London. We've seen him! Twice!"

That made Snape sit up. "Where?"

"He was at the circus. He was in the crowd. We saw him about a minute before Boris was killed. And he was at the cemetery. Not underground—on top of it! I followed him and he ran away."

"How do you know it was Smile?" Snape asked.

"I don't. At least, I can't be sure. But I've seen a photo-graph of him and it looked the same."

"We don't know much about Smile," Snape admitted. "Henderson was watching the apartment, but he only saw him once. We know when he was born and when he died. But that's about all . . ."

"He didn't die. I'm telling you. Dig up the coffin and you'll probably find it's empty!"

Snape looked at Boyle, then back at me. Slowly, he nodded. "All right, laddy," he said. "Let's play it your way. But if you're wasting my time . . . it's your funeral!"

I'll tell you now. There's one place you don't want to be at five past twelve on a black November night—and that's in a cemetery. The ground was so cold I could feel it all the way up to my knees, and every time I breathed the ice seemed to find its way into my skull. There were the four of us there— Snape, Boyle, Tim, and myself—and now we'd been joined by another half-dozen police officers and workmen, two of whom were operating a mechanical digger that whined and groaned as it clawed at the frozen earth. Tim was whining and groaning, too, as a matter of fact. I think he'd have pre- ferred to have been in bed.

But maybe it wasn't just the weather that was managing to chill me. The whole thing was like a scene out of *Frankenstein*. You know the one—where Igor the deformed Hungarian servant has to climb into the grave and steal a human brain. Glancing at Boyle, I saw a distinct physical resemblance. I had to remind myself that two days ago I had been enjoying vaca- tion and that the following day I would be back at school, with all the fun of honors geography and French. In the meantime I had somehow stumbled into a horror film. I wondered what was going to turn up in the final reel.

The digger stabbed down. The earth shifted. Gradually the hole got deeper. There was a clunk—metal hitting wood—and two of the workmen climbed in to clear away the rest of the soil with spades. Snape moved forward.

I didn't watch as the coffin was opened. You have to remember that I was only thirteen years old, and if someone had made a film out of what was going on here, I wouldn't even have been allowed to see it.

"Boyle!" Snape muttered the single word and the other man lowered himself into the hole. There was a pause. Then . . .

"Sir!"

Boyle was holding something. He passed it up to Snape. It was dark blue, shaped a bit like a bell, only paper-thin. There was a silver disc squashed in the middle. It took me a few seconds to work out what it was. Then I realized. It was a police officer's helmet. But one that had been flattened.

"Henderson!" Snape muttered.

There had been a police officer watching Smile's apartment. He had disappeared a week before the accident. His name had been Henderson.

And now we knew what had happened to him.

"Don't you see, Tim? It was Henderson who was killed. Not Lenny Smile!"

The two of us were back at our Camden apartment. After our hours spent in the cemetery, we were too cold to go to bed. I'd made us both hot chocolate and Tim was wearing two pairs of pajamas and two robes, with a hot-water bottle clasped to his chest.

"But who killed him?"

"Lenny Smile."

"But what about Hoover? And the woman? They were there when it happened."

For once, Tim was right. Rodney Hoover and Fiona Lee must have been part of it. Snape had already gone to arrest them. The man they had helped down the stairs must have been Henderson. I had been right about that. He had been drugged. They had taken him out of the apartment and thrown him into the road, just as Barry Krishner turned the corner on his way home . . .

And yet it wasn't going to be easy to prove. There were no witnesses. And until Smile was found, it was hard to see exactly what he could do. Suddenly I realized how clever Smile had been. The blurred man? He had been more than that. He had run Dream Time, he had stolen all the money, and he had remained virtually invisible.

"Nobody knew him." I said.

"Who?"

"Smile. Mrs. Lovely never spoke to him. Joe Carter only wrote to him. We went to his apartment and it was like he'd never actually lived there. Even Rodney Hoover and Fiona Lee couldn't tell us much about him."

Tim nodded. I yawned. It was two o'clock, way past my

bedtime. And in just five and a half hours I'd be getting ready for school. Monday was going to be a long day.

"You'll have to go to the Ritz tomorrow," I said.

"Why?"

"To tell Joe Carter about his so-called best friend."

Tim sighed. "It's not going to be easy," he said. "He had this big idea about Lenny Smile when all the time he was someone else!"

I finished my hot chocolate and stood up. Then, suddenly, it hit me. "What did you just say?" I asked.

"I've forgotten." Tim was so tired he was forgetting what he was saying even as he said it.

"Someone else! That's exactly the point! Of course!"

There had been so many clues. The note in the cemetery. Mrs. Lovely and the card Lenny had sent her. The gravestone. The photograph of Smile outside the Café Debussy. And Snape . . .

"We know when he was born . . ."

But it was only now, when I was almost too tired to move, that it came together. The truth. All of it.

The following morning, I didn't go to school. Instead I made two telephone calls, and then later on, just after ten o'clock, Tim and I set out for the final showdown.

It was time to meet Lenny Smile.

THE BIG WHEEL

The subway from Camden Town to Waterloo is express on the Northern line—which was probably just as well. I'd only had about five hours' sleep, and I was so tired that the whole world seemed to be shimmering and moving in slow motion. Tim was just as bad. He had a terrible nightmare in which he was lowered, still standing up, into Lenny's grave—and woke up screaming. I suppose it wasn't too surprising. He'd fallen asleep on the escalator.

But the two of us had livened up a little by the time we'd reached the other end. The weather had taken a turn for the worse. The rain was sheeting down, sucking any color or warmth out of the city. We had left Waterloo Station behind us, making for the South Bank, a stretch of London that has trouble looking beautiful even on the sunniest day. This is where you'll find the National Theatre and the National Film Theatre, both designed by architects with huge buckets of prefabricated cement. There weren't many people around. Just a few commuters struggling with umbrellas that the wind had turned inside out. Tim and I hurried forward without speaking. The rain lashed down, hit the concrete, and bounced up again, wetting us twice.

I had made the telephone call just after breakfast.

"Mrs. Lee?"

"Yes. Who is this?" Fiona Lee's clipped vowels had been instantly recognizable down the line.

"This is Nick Diamond. Remember me?"

A pause.

"I want to meet with Lenny Smile."

A longer pause. Then, "That's not possible. Lenny Smile is dead."

"You're lying. You know where he is. I want to see the three of you. Hoover, Lenny, and you. Eleven o'clock at the London Eye. And if you don't want me to go to the police, you'd better not be late."

You've probably seen the London Eye, the huge Ferris wheel they put up outside County Hall. It's one of the big surprises of modern London. Unlike the Millennium Dome, it has actually been a success. It opened on time. It worked. It didn't fall over. At the end of the millennium year they decided to keep it, and suddenly it was part of London—a brilliant silver circle at once huge and yet somehow fragile. Tim had taken me on it for my thirteenth birthday and we'd enjoyed the view so much we'd gone a second time. Well, as they say, one good turn deserves another.

Not that we were going to see much today. The clouds were so low that the cars at the top almost seemed to disappear into them. You could see the Houses of Parliament on the other side of the river and, hazy in the distance, St. Paul's. But that was about it. If there was a single day in the year

when it wasn't worth paying ten dollars for the ride, this was
it, which would explain why there were no crowds around
when we approached: just Rodney Hoover and Fiona Lee,
both wearing raincoats, waiting for us to arrive.

There was no sign of Lenny Smile, but I wasn't surprised. I had known he would never show up.

"Why are you calling us?" Hoover demanded. "First we
have the police accusing us of terrible things. Then you,
wanting to see Lenny. We don't know where Lenny is! As far
as we know, he's dead . . ."

"Why don't we get out of the rain?" I suggested. "How
about the wheel?" It seemed like a good idea. The rain was
still bucketing down and there was nowhere else to go.

"After you, Mr. Hoover . . ."

We bought tickets and climbed into the first compartment that came around. I wasn't surprised to find that there
would only be the four of us in it for this turn of the wheel.
The doors slid shut, and slowly—so slowly that we barely
knew we were moving—we were carried up into the sky,
into the driving rain.

There was a pause as if nobody knew quite what to say.
Then Fiona broke the silence. "We already told that ghastly
little policeman . . . Detective Chief Inspector Snape. Lenny
was with us that day. He was killed by the steamroller. And
it is Lenny buried in the cemetery."

"No it isn't," I said. "Lenny Smile is right here now. He's
on the big wheel. Inside this compartment."

"Is he?" Tim looked under the seat. "I don't see him!"

"That's because you're not looking in the right place, Tim," I said. "But that was the whole idea. You said it yourself last night. We all thought Lenny Smile was one thing, but in fact he was something else."

"You are not making the lot of sense," Hoover said. His face, dark to begin with, had gone darker. He was watching me with nervous eyes.

"I should have known from the start that there was something strange about Lenny Smile," I said. "Nothing about him added up. Nobody—except you—had ever seen him. And everything about him was a lie."

"You mean . . . his name wasn't Lenny Smile?" Tim asked.

"Lenny Smile never existed, Tim!" I explained. "He was a fantasy. I should have known when I saw the details on the gravestone. It said that he was born on April 31, 1955. But that was the first lie. There are only thirty days in April. April 31 doesn't exist!"

"It was a mistake . . ." Fiona muttered.

"Maybe. But then there was that photograph Carter showed us of 'Lenny' standing outside the Café Debussy. You told us that he was allergic to a lot of things, and one of those things was animals. But in the photograph there's a cat sitting between his feet—and he doesn't seem to care. The allergy business was a lie. But it was a clever one. It meant that he had a reason not to be seen. He had to stay indoors because he was ill . . ."

Inch by inch, the big wheel carried us farther away from the ground. The rain was hammering against the glass. Looking out, I could barely see the buildings on the north bank of the river. There was Big Ben, but then the rain swept across it, turning it into a series of brown and white streaks.

Tim gaped. "So there was no Lenny Smile!" he exclaimed.

"That's right. Except when Hoover *pretended* to be Lenny Smile. Don't you see? He rented the apartment even though he never actually lived there. Occasionally he went in and out to make it look as if there was someone there. And of course it was Hoover who wrote that letter to Mrs. Lovely."

"How do you know?"

"Because it was written in green ink. The message we saw in the card on Lenny's grave was also written in green ink—and it was the same handwriting. I should have seen from the start. It was Hoover we saw at the circus. And he was also there at Brompton Cemetery the day we visited the grave. I should have known it was him as soon as we met him at the Dream Time office."

"Why?" Tim asked.

"Because Hoover had never met us—but somehow he knew we'd been to Brompton Cemetery. Don't you remember what he said to us? 'You know very well that he's lying there in Brompton Cemetery.' Those were his exact words. But he only knew we knew because he knew who we were, and he knew who we were because he'd seen us!"

Tim scratched his head. "Could you say that last bit again?"

Fiona looked at me scornfully. "You're talking nonsense!" she said. "Why would Rodney and I want to invent a man called Lenny Smile?" she continued.

"Because the two of you were stealing millions of dollars from Dream Time. You knew that eventually the police would catch up with you. And there was always the danger that someone like Joe Carter would come over from America to find out what was happening to his money. You were the brains behind the charity. You were the 'big wheels,' if you like. But you needed someone to take the blame and then disappear. That was Lenny Smile. Henderson—the policeman—must have found out what was going on, so he had to die, too. And that was your brilliant idea. You'd turn Henderson into Lenny Smile. He went under the steamroller and, as far as you were concerned, that was the end of the matter. Smile was dead. There was nothing left to investigate."

The car was still moving up. There were a few pedestrians out on the South Bank. By now they were no more than dots.

"But now the police think Lenny Smile is alive," I went on. "That's why the two of you aren't in jail. They're looking for him. They don't have any proof against you. So the two of you are in the clear!"

Hoover had listened to all this in silence but now he smiled, his thin lips peeling back from his teeth. "You have it exactly right," he said. "Fiona and I are nobodies. We were just working for Lenny Smile. He is the real crook. And, as you say, they have no proof. Nobody has any proof."

"Hoover dressed up as Lenny Smile . . ." Tim was still trying to work it all out.

"Only once. For the photograph that Joe Carter requested. But he was wearing the same coat and the same gloves when we saw him—which is why we thought he was Lenny Smile. Both times, he was too far away for us to see his face. And, of course, in the photograph the face was purposely blurred." I turned to Rodney. "I'd be interested to know, though. What were you doing in the cemetery?"

Hoover shrugged. "I realized that the bloody fool of an undertaker had made a mistake with the date on the gravestone. I went there to put it right. When I saw you and your brother at the grave, I knew something was wrong. I have to admit, I panicked. And ran."

"And the circus . . . ?"

"Mrs. Lovely told us there had been a witness. I had to track him down and make sure he didn't talk."

"But it wouldn't have mattered if he'd talked," Tim said. "He was Russian! Nobody would have understood."

"I don't believe in taking chances," Rodney said. His hand had slid into his coat pocket. Why wasn't I surprised, when it came out, to see that it was holding a gun?

"He's got a gun!" Tim squealed.

"That's right, Tim," I said.

"You've been very clever," Hoover snarled. "But you haven't quite thought it through." He glanced out of the window. We had reached the top of the circle, as high up as the Ferris wheel went. Suddenly Hoover fired. The glass door smashed. Tim leaped. The rain came rushing in. "An unfortunate accident!" Hoover shouted above the howl of the wind. "The door malfunctioned. Somehow it broke. You and your brother fell out."

"No we didn't!" Tim whimpered.

"Anyway, by the time they've finished wiping you off the South Bank, Fiona and I will have disappeared. The money is in a nice little bank in Brazil. We'll move there. A beach house in Rio de Janeiro! We'll live a life of luxury."

"That money was meant for sick children!" I shouted. "Don't you have any shame at all?"

"I cannot afford shame!" He gestured with the gun, pointing at the shattered glass and the swirling rain. "Now which one of you is going to step out first?"

"He is!" Tim pointed at me.

"No, I'm not," I said. I turned back to Hoover. "It won't work, Hoover. Why don't you take a look in the next car?"

Hoover's eyes narrowed. Fiona Lee went over to the window. There were about twenty people in the car above us on the London Eye. All of them were dressed in blue. "It's full of policemen!" she exclaimed. She went over to the other side. "And the one below us! That's full of police, too!"

"It must be their day off!" Tim said.

"Forget it, Tim." It was my turn to smile. "You've been set up, Hoover. Every word you've said has been recorded. The car's bugged. Your confession is on tape right now, and as soon as the ride is over, you and Fiona will have another ride. To jail!"

Fiona had begun to tremble. Hoover's eyes twitched. His grip tightened on the gun. "Maybe I'll kill you anyway," he said. "Just for the fun of it . . ."

And that was when the helicopter appeared—a dark blue police helicopter, its blades beating at the rain outside the broken window. It had come swooping out of the clouds and now hovered just a few feet away. I could see Snape in the passenger seat. Boyle was in the back, dressed in a flak jacket, cradling an automatic rifle. I just hoped he was pointing it at Hoover, not at Tim.

"Why do you think the police released you?" I shouted above the noise of the helicopter. "I called Snape this morning and told him what I'd worked out and he asked me to meet you. You walked into a trap. He knew you'd feel safe up in the air, just the four of us. He wanted you to confess."

A second later there was a crackle and Snape's voice came, amplified, from the helicopter. "Put the gun down, Hoover! The car is surrounded!"

Hoover swore in Ukrainian, and before I could stop him he had twisted around and fired at the helicopter.

I threw myself at Hoover.

He fired a second time. But his aim had gone wild. The

bullet hit Fiona in the shoulder. She screamed and fell to her knees.

Hoover, with my hands at his throat, crashed into the window. This one didn't break. I heard the toughened glass clunk against his un-toughened skull. His eyes glazed and he slid to the ground.

I turned to Tim. "Are you all right, Tim?" I asked.

"Yes, I'm fine." He pointed past the helicopter. "Look! You can see Trafalgar Square!"

It took another fifteen minutes for the car to reach the ground. At once we were surrounded by uniformed police officers. Hoover and Lee were dragged out. They'd spend a few days in hospital on their way to jail. The helicopter with Snape and Boyle in was nowhere to be seen. With a bit of luck a strong gust of wind would have blown it out of London and maybe into Essex. The trouble with those two was that no matter how many times we helped them, they'd never thank us. And I'd probably end up with a detention for missing a day of school.

"We'd better go to the Ritz," I said.

"For dinner?" Tim asked.

"No, Tim. Joe Carter . . ."

The American was still waiting to hear about his best friend, Lenny Smile. I wasn't looking forward to breaking the bad news to him. Maybe I'd leave that to Tim. After all, discreet was his middle name.

It had stopped raining. Tim and I walked along the South Bank, leaving the London Eye behind us. There were workmen ahead of us, shoveling a rich, black ooze onto the surface of the road. On the pavement, a tramp stood with an upturned hat, playing some sort of plinky-plonk music on a strange instrument—a zither, I think. I found a dollar and dropped it into the hat. Charity. That was how this had all begun.

"Tar!" the tramp warned, pointing ahead.

"Don't mention it," Tim said. His foot splashed down in a puddle of it. We crossed the river, the sound of the zither fading into the distance behind.

THE FRENCH
CONFECTION

CONTENTS

THE FRENCH FOR MURDER

Everybody loves Paris. There's an old guy who even wrote a song about it. "I love Paris in the springtime . . ."; that's how it goes. Well, all I can say is, he obviously never went there with my big brother, Tim. I did—and it almost killed me.

It all started with a strawberry yogurt.

It was a French strawberry yogurt, of course, and it was all we had in the fridge for breakfast. Tim and I tossed a coin to decide who'd get the first mouthful. Then we tossed the coin to see who'd keep the coin. Tim won both times. So there I was sitting at the breakfast table chewing my nails, which was all I had to chew, when Tim suddenly let out a great gurgle and started waving his spoon in the air like he was trying to swat a fly.

"What is it, Tim?" I asked. "Don't tell me! You've found a strawberry!"

"No, Nick! Look . . . !"

He was holding up the silver foil that he'd just torn off the yogurt container and looking at it, and now I understood. The company that made the yogurt was having one of those promotions. You've probably seen them on chocolate bars or chips or Coke cans. These days you can't even open a can of beans without finding out if you've won a car or a vacation in Mexico or a check for a thousand dollars. Personally, I'm just grateful if I actually find some beans. Anyway, the yogurt people were offering a whole range of prizes and there it was, written on the underside of the foil.

Congratulations from Bestlé Fruit Yogurts! You have just won a weekend for two in Paris! Just telephone the number printed on the container for further details and . . . Bon Voyage!

"I've won, Nick!" Tim gasped. "A weekend for two . . . !" He stopped and bit his thumb. "Who shall I take?" he muttered.

"Oh, thanks a lot, Tim," I said. "It was me who bought the yogurt."

"But it was my money."

"If it hadn't been for me, you'd have spent it on a Popsicle."

Tim scowled. "But Paris, Nick! It's the most romantic city in Europe. I want to take my girlfriend."

"Tim," I reminded him. "You haven't got a girlfriend."

That was a bit cruel of me. The truth was, Tim hadn't been very lucky in love. His first serious relationship had ended tragically when his girlfriend had tried to murder him. After that he'd replied to one of those advertisements in the lonely hearts column of a newspaper, but he couldn't have read it properly because the girl had turned out to be a guy who spent the evening chasing him around Paddington station. His last girlfriend had been a fire-eater in a local circus. He'd taken her out for a romantic, candlelit dinner but she'd completely spoiled it by eating the candles. Right now he was on his own. He sometimes said he felt like a monk—but without the haircut or the religion.

Anyway, we argued a bit more but finally he picked up the telephone and rang the number on the yogurt container. There was no answer.

"That's because you've telephoned the sell-by date," I told him. I turned the carton over. "This is the number here . . ."

And that was how, three weeks later, we found ourselves standing in the lobby of Waterloo station. Tim was carrying the tickets. I was carrying the bags. It had been more than a year since we'd been abroad—that had been to Amsterdam on the trail of the mysterious assassin known as Charon—and that time we had gone by ferry. Tim had been completely seasick even before he reached the sea. I was relieved that this time we were going by train, taking the Channel Tunnel, although with Tim, of course, you never knew.

We took the escalator down to the international terminal. Ahead of us, the tunnel was waiting: a thirty-two-mile stretch linking England and France, built at a cost of twelve billion dollars.

"You have to admit," Tim said. "It's an engineering marvel."

"That's just what I was thinking," I said.

"Yes. It's a fantastic escalator. And so much faster than going down the stairs . . ."

We had two seats next to each other right in the middle of one of the carriages. The train was pretty full and soon we were joined by two other passengers opposite us. They were both traveling alone. The first was from Texas—you could tell just from his hat. He was chewing an unlit cigar (this was a nonsmoking compartment) and reading a magazine: *International Oil*. The other passenger was a very old lady with white hair and skin so wrinkled I was amazed it managed to stay on. I wasn't sure if she had huge eyes or extremely powerful glasses but every time she looked at me I thought I was about to be hit by a pair of gray-and-white golf balls. I looked out of the window. The platform was already empty, sweeping in a graceful curve beneath the great glass canopy. Somewhere a door slammed.

The train left exactly on time at ten minutes past ten. There was no whistle. No announcement. I wouldn't have known we had moved if it hadn't been for the slight shudder— and even that was Tim, not the train. He was obviously excited.

About an hour later there was an announcement on the intercom and we dipped into the tunnel carved out underneath the sea. That was a nonevent, too. A parking lot, a sign advertising hamburgers, a white cement wall, and suddenly the outside world disappeared, replaced by rushing blackness. So this was the engineering miracle of the last century? As far as Eurostar was concerned, it was just a hole in the ground.

Tim had been ready with his camera and now he drew back, disappointed. "Is this it?" he demanded.

I looked up from my book. "What were you expecting, Tim?" I asked.

"I thought this train went underwater!" Tim sighed. "I wanted to take some pictures of the fish!"

The other passengers had heard this and somehow it broke the silence. The old lady had been knitting what looked like a multicolored sack but now she looked up. "I love taking the train," she announced, and for the first time I realized that she was French. Her accent was so thick you could have wrapped yourself in it to keep warm.

"It sure is one hell of a thing," the Texan agreed. "London to Paris in three and a half hours. Great for business."

The Texan held up his magazine. "I'm in oil. Jed Mathis is the name."

"Why do you call your oil Jed Mathis?" Tim asked.

"I'm sorry?" Jed looked confused. He turned to the old lady. "Are you visiting your grandchildren in Paris?" he asked.

"*Non!*" the lady replied.

Tim dug into his pocket and pulled out a French dictionary. While he was looking up the word, she continued in English.

"I have a little cake shop in Paris. Erica Nice. That's my name. Please, you must try some of my almond slices." And before anyone could stop her, she'd pulled out a bag of cakes that she offererd to us all.

We were still hurtling through the darkness. Tim put away his dictionary and helped himself. At the same time, a steward approached us, pushing one of those trolleys piled up with sandwiches and coffee. He was a thin, pale man with a drooping mustache and slightly sunken eyes. The name on his badge was Marc Chabrol. I remember thinking even then that he looked nervous. A nervous traveler, I thought. But then, why would a nervous traveler work on a train?

Jed produced a wallet full of dollars and offered to buy us all coffee. A free breakfast and we hadn't even arrived. Things were definitely looking up.

"So what do you do?" Erica Nice asked, turning to Tim.

Tim gave a crooked smile. It was meant to make him look smart but in fact he just looked as though he had a toothache. "I'm a private detective," he said.

The steward dropped one of the coffee cups. Fortunately, he hadn't added the water yet. Coffee granules showered over the Kit Kats.

"A private detective?" Erica trilled. "How very unusual!"

"Are you going to Paris on business?" the Texan asked.

Now of course the answer was no. We were on vacation. Tim hadn't had any business for several weeks and even then he had only been hired to find a missing dog. In fact he had spent three days at Battersea Dogs' Home, where he had been bitten three times—twice by dogs. The trouble was, though, he was never going to admit this. He liked to think of himself as a man of mystery. So now he winked and leaned forward. "Just between you and me," he drawled, "I'm on a case." Yes. A nutcase, I thought. But he went on. "I've been hired by Interplop."

"You mean Interpol," the Texan said.

"The International Police," Tim agreed. "It's a top-secret case. It's so secret, they don't even know about it at the top. In other words—" he gestured with his almond slice, spraying Jed with crumbs— ". . . a case for Tim Diamond."

The steward had obviously heard all this. As he put down the first cup of coffee, his hands were shaking so much that the liquid spilled over the table. His face had been pale to begin with. Now it had no color at all. Even his mustache seemed to have faded.

"Where are you staying in Paris?" the old lady asked.

"It's a hotel called The Fat Greek," Tim said.

"Le Chat Gris," I corrected him. It was French for "gray cat" and this was the name of the hotel where Bestlé Yogurts had booked us for three nights.

The name seemed to have an electric effect on the steward. I'd been watching him out of the corner of my eye and actually saw him step backward, colliding with the trolley. The bottles and cans shook. Two packages of ginger-bread cookies rocketed onto the floor. The man was terrified. But why?

"Paris is so beautiful in the spring," the old lady said. She'd obviously seen the effect that Tim was having on the steward and perhaps she was trying to change the subject before the poor man had a heart attack. "You must make sure you take a stroll on the Champs-Élysées . . . if you have the time."

"How much do I owe you for the coffee?" the American asked.

"Six euros, monsieur . . ." The steward reached down and picked up the cookies. The way he took the money and moved off, he could have been trying to get to Paris ahead of the train. I guessed he wanted to get away from us as fast as he could. And I was right. He didn't even stop to offer anyone else in the carriage a coffee. He simply disappeared. Later, when I went to the men's room, I saw the trolley standing on its own in the passageway.

Twenty minutes after we'd entered the tunnel, the train burst out again. There was nothing to show that we'd left one country and entered another. The French cows grazing in the fields looked just the same as the English ones on the other side. An official came past, looking at passports. Erica Nice looked at Tim as if puzzled in some way and went back to her knitting. Jed returned to his magazine. We didn't speak for the rest of the journey.

We arrived at the Gare du Nord train station about an hour later. As everyone struggled with their luggage, Tim gazed at the name. "When do we arrive in Paris?" he asked.

"Tim, this is Paris," I told him. "The Gare du Nord means north station. There are lots of stations in the city."

"I hope you have a lovely time," Erica Nice said. She had

an old carpetbag. It was big enough to hold a carpet—and maybe that was what she had been knitting. She winked at Tim. "Good luck with the case, *mon ami!*"

Meanwhile, the Texan had grabbed a leather briefcase. He nodded at us briefly and joined the line for the exit. Tim and I retrieved our two bags and a few moments later we were standing on the platform, wondering which way to go.

"We'd better find the metro," I said. Bestlé had given us some spending money for the weekend but I didn't think it would be enough for us to travel everywhere by taxi.

Tim shook his head. "Forget the metro, Nick," he said. "Let's take the subway."

I didn't even bother to argue. I knew a little French—I'd been learning it from a little Frenchman who taught at our school—and I knew, for example, that metro was the French word for subway. On the other hand, I didn't know the French for idiot, which was the English word for Tim. I picked up the bags and prepared to follow him when suddenly we found ourselves interrupted.

It was Marc Chabrol. The French steward had reappeared and was standing in front of us, blocking our way. He was terrified. I could see it in his bulging eyes, the sweat on his cheeks, the yellow-and-black bow tie that had climbed halfway up his neck.

"I have to talk to you, monsieur," he rasped. He was speaking in English, the words as uncomfortable in his mouth as somebody else's false teeth. "Tonight. At eleven o'clock. There is a café in the sixth *arrondissement*. It is called La Palette . . ."

"That's very nice of you," Tim said. He seemed to think that Chabrol was inviting us out for a drink.

"Beware of the mad American!" The steward whispered the words as if he were too afraid to speak them aloud. "The mad American . . . !"

He was about to add something but then his face changed again. He seemed to freeze as if his worst nightmare had just come true. I glanced left and right, but if there was someone he had recognized in the crowd, I didn't see them. *"Oh mon Dieu!"* he whispered. He seized Tim's hand and pressed something into the palm. Then he turned and staggered away.

Tim opened his hand. He was holding a small blue envelope with a gold star printed on the side. I recognized it at once. It was a packet of sugar from the train. "What was all that about?" Tim asked.

I took the sugar and examined it. I thought he might have written something on it—a telephone number or something. But it was just a little bag of sugar. I slipped it into my back pocket. "I don't know . . ." I said. And I didn't. Why should the steward have left us with a spoonful of sugar? Why did he want to meet us later that night? What was going on?

"Funny people, the French," Tim said.

Ten minutes later, we were still at the Gare du Nord. The money that Bestlé had given us was in dollars. We needed euros and that meant lining up at the Bureau de Change. The line was a long one and it seemed to be moving at a rate of one euro per hour.

We had just reached the window when we heard the scream.

It was like no sound I had ever heard, thin and high and horribly final. The station was huge and noisy but the scream cut through the crowd like a scalpel. Everybody stopped and turned to see where it had come from. Even Tim heard it. "Oh dear," he said. "It sounds like someone has stepped on a cat."

Tim changed thirty dollars, and taking the money, we moved in the direction of the metro. Already a police car had arrived and several uniformed guards were hurrying toward the trains. I strained to hear what the crowd was saying. They were speaking French, of course. That didn't make it any easier.

"What's happened?"

"It's terrible. Somebody has fallen under a train."

"It was a steward. He was on the train from London. He fell off a platform."

"Is he hurt?"

"He's dead. Crushed by a train."

I heard all of it. I understood some of it. I didn't like any of it. A steward? Off the London train? Somehow I didn't need to ask his name.

"Tim," I asked, "what's the French for murder?"

Tim shrugged. "Why do you want to know?"

"I don't know." I stepped onto the escalator and allowed it to carry me down. "I've just got a feeling it's something we're going to need."

LE CHAT GRIS

Le Chat Gris was in the Latin Quarter, a dark, busy area on the south side of the River Seine. Here the streets were full of students and the smell of cheap food. It was a small, narrow building, wedged between an art gallery and a café. A metal cat, more rusty than gray, hung over the main entrance and there were brightly colored flowers in the front windows. On closer inspection they turned out to be made of plastic.

The reception area was so small that if you went in too quickly you'd be out the other side. There was a receptionist standing behind the desk, which was just as well as there wasn't enough room for a chair. He was an old man, at least sixty, with a crumpled face and something terribly wrong with his eyes. When he looked at our passports he had to hold them up beside his ear. He took our names, then sent us to a room on the fifth floor. Fortunately there was an elevator but it wasn't much bigger than a telephone booth. Tim and I stood shoulder to shoulder with our suitcases as it creaked and trembled slowly up. Next time, I decided, I'd take the stairs.

The truth was that Bestlé hadn't been too generous with the accommodation. Our room was built into the roof with wooden beams that sloped down at strange angles. It made me think of the Hunchback of Notre Dame. You needed a hunched back to avoid hitting your head on the ceiling. There were two beds, a single window with a view over the other rooftops, a chest of drawers, and a bathroom too small to take a bath in.

"Which bed do you want?" I asked.

"This one!" Tim threw himself onto the bed next to the window. There was a loud *ping* as several of the springs snapped. I sat down, more carefully, on the other bed. It felt like the quilt wasn't just filled with goose feathers, but they'd also left in half the goose.

We dumped our luggage and went out. This was, after all, Thursday morning and we only had until Sunday afternoon. Back in the reception area, the receptionist was talking to a new arrival. This was a square-shouldered man with narrow eyes and black, slicked-back hair. He was wearing an expensive, charcoal gray suit. Both of them stopped when they saw us. I dropped the key with a clunk.

"*Merci,*" I said.

Neither of the men said anything. Maybe it was my accent.

There was a mirror next to the front door and but for that I wouldn't have noticed what happened next. But as Tim and I made our way out, the man in the gray suit reached out and took my key, turning it around so that he could read the number. He was interested in us. That was for sure. His eyes, empty of emotion, were still scrutinizing us as the door swung shut and we found ourselves in the street.

First the whispered warning: *"Beware the mad American!"* Then the death of the steward from the train. And now this. There was a nasty smell in the air and already I knew it wasn't just French cheese.

"Which way, Nick?" Tim was waiting for me, holding a camera. He had already taken three photographs of the hotel, a streetlamp, and a mailbox and he was waiting for me in the morning sunlight. I wondered if he had remembered to put in film.

I thought for a moment. I was probably being stupid. We were here in Paris for the weekend and nothing was going to happen. I couldn't even be sure that it really was Marc Chabrol who had fallen under the train. "Let's try down there," I said, pointing down the street.

"Good idea," Tim agreed as he turned the other way.

What can I tell you about Paris? I'm no travel writer. I'm not crazy about writing and I can't usually afford to travel. But anyway . . .

Paris is a big city full of French people. It's a lot prettier than London and for that matter so are the people. They're everywhere: in the street-side cafés, sipping black coffee from thimble-sized cups, strolling along the Seine in their designer sunglasses, snapping at one another on the bridges through eighteen inches of the latest Japanese lens. The streets are narrower than in London and looking at the traffic you get the feeling that war has broken out. There are cars parked everywhere. On the streets and on the sidewalks. Actually, it's hard to tell which cars are parked and which ones are just stuck in the traffic jams. But the strange thing is that nobody seems to be in a hurry. Life is just a big jumble that moves along at its own pace, and if you're in a hurry to leave then maybe you should never have come there in the first place.

That first day, Tim and I did the usual tourist things. We went up the Eiffel Tower. Tim fainted. So we came down again. We went to the cathedral of Notre Dame and I took a picture of Tim and another of a gargoyle. I just hoped that when I got them developed I'd remember which was which. We went up the Champs-Élysées and down the Jardin des Tuileries. By lunchtime, my stomach was rumbling. So, more worryingly, were my feet.

We had an early supper at a brasserie overlooking another brasserie. That's another thing about Paris. There are brasseries everywhere. Tim ordered two ham sandwiches, a beer for him, and a Coke for me. Then I ordered them again using words the waiter understood. The sandwiches arrived: eight inches of bread, I noticed, but only four inches of ham.

"This is the life, eh, Nick?" Tim sighed as he sipped his beer.

"Yes, Tim," I said. "And this is the bill."

Tim glanced at it and swallowed his beer the wrong way. "Ten euros!" he exclaimed. "That's . . . that's . . . !" He frowned. "How much is that?"

"A euro's worth about seven old francs," I explained. "It's about a dollar fifty. So the bill is about fifteen dollars."

Tim shook his head. "I hate this new money," he said.

"I know," I agreed. "Because you haven't got any."

We were walking back in the direction of the hotel when it happened. We were in one of those quiet, antique streets near the Seine when two men appeared, blocking our way. The first was in his forties, tall and slim, wearing a white linen suit that was so crumpled and dirty, it hung off him like a used paper bag. He was one of the ugliest men I had ever seen. He had green eyes, a small nose, and a mouth like a knife wound. None of these were in quite the right place. It was as if his whole face had been drawn by a six-year-old child.

His partner was about twenty years younger with the body of an ape and, if the dull glimmer in his eyes was anything to go by, a brain to match. He was wearing jeans and a leather jacket and smoking a cigarette. I guessed he was a bodybuilder. He had muscles bulging everywhere and a neck that somehow managed to be wider than his head. His hair was blond and greasy. He had fat lips and a tiny beard sprouting out of the middle of his chin.

"Good evening," White Suit said in perfect English. His voice came out like a whisper from a punctured balloon. "My name is Bastille. Jacques Bastille. My friend's name is Lavache. I wonder if I might speak with you."

"If you want to know the way, don't ask us!" Tim replied. "We're lost, too."

"I'm not lost. Oh, no." Bastille smiled, revealing teeth the color of French mustard. "No. But I want to know what he told you. I want to know what you know."

Tim turned to me, puzzled.

"What exactly do you mean?" I asked.

"The steward on the train. What did he tell you?" There was a pause. "Lavache!"

Bastille nodded and his partner produced what looked like a little model of that famous statue, the *Venus de Milo*. You know the one. The naked woman with no arms that stands somewhere in the Louvre.

"No thank you," Tim began. "We're not . . ."

Lavache pressed a button and four inches of razor-sharp metal sprang out of the head of the statue. It was a neat trick. I don't think the real statue ever did that.

Tim stared at it.

"Where is it?" Bastille demanded.

"Your friend's holding it in his hand!" Tim gasped.

"Not the knife! *Sacré bleu!* Are all the English such idiots? I am talking about the object. The item that you were given this morning at the Gare du Nord."

"I wasn't given anything!" Tim wailed.

"It's true," I said, even though I knew that it wasn't.

Bastille blinked heavily. "You're lying."

"No, we're not," Tim replied. "Cross my heart and hope to—"

"Tim!" I interrupted.

"Kill them both!" Bastille snapped.

They really did mean to kill us there and then in that quiet Paris street. Lavache lifted the knife, his stubby fingers curving around the base, a bead of saliva glistening at the corner of his mouth. I glanced back, wondering if we could run. But it was hopeless. We'd be cut down before we could take a step.

"The older one first," Bastille commanded.

"That's him!" Tim said, pointing at me.

"Tim!" I exclaimed.

The knife hovered between us.

But then suddenly a party of American tourists turned the corner—about twenty of them, following a guide who was holding an umbrella with a Stars and Stripes attached to the tip. They were jabbering excitedly as they descended on us. There was nothing Bastille and Lavache could do. Suddenly they were surrounded, and realizing this was our only chance I grabbed hold of Tim and moved away, keeping a wall of American tourists between us and our attackers. Only when we'd come to the top of the street where it joined the wide and busy Boulevard St. Michel did we break away and run.

But the two killers weren't going to let us get away quite so easily. I glanced back and saw them pushing their way through the crowd. Bastille shoved out a hand and one of the tourists, an elderly woman, shrieked and fell backward into a fountain. Several of the other tourists stopped and took photographs of her. Bastille stepped into the road. A car swerved to avoid him and crashed into the front of a restaurant. Two lobsters and a plateful of mussels were sent flying. Someone screamed.

It still wasn't dark. The streets were full of people on their way to restaurants, too wrapped up in their own affairs to notice two English visitors running for their lives. I had no idea where I was going and I wasn't going to stop and ask for directions. I grabbed Tim again and steered him up an alleyway with dozens more restaurants on both sides. A waiter in a long white apron, carrying several trays laden with plates and glasses, stepped out in front of me. There was no way I could avoid him. There was a strangled cry, then a crash.

"*Excusez-moi!*" Tim burbled.

Fortunately, I didn't know enough French to understand the waiter's reply.

The alleyway brought us back to the Seine. I could see Notre Dame in the distance. Only a few hours before we had been standing on one of its towers, enjoying the view. How could our vacation have become a nightmare so quickly?

"This way, Tim!" I shouted.

I pulled him across a busy street, cars screeching to a halt, horns blaring. A policeman turned around to face us, a whistle clenched between his teeth, his hands scrabbling for his gun. I swear he would have shot us except that we were already on the other side of the road and a few seconds later

Bastille had reached him, brutally pushing him out of the way. The unfortunate cop spun around and collided with a cyclist. Both of them collapsed in a tangle of rubber and steel. The last I saw of the cop, he had gotten back to his feet and was shouting at us, making a curious, high-pitched noise. Evidently he had swallowed his whistle, which had now gotten lodged in his throat.

The river was now right in front of us with a pedestrian bridge leading over to the other side. Bastille and Lavache were already crossing the road, blocked for a moment by a bus that had slipped in between them and us.

"The river!" I said.

Tim reached into his pocket and took out his camera.

"No!" I yelled. "I don't want you to photograph it! I want us to cross it!"

We ran onto the bridge, but I hadn't taken more than a few steps before I saw that we'd made a bad mistake. The bridge was closed. There was a tall barrier running across the middle of it with a MEN AT WORK sign—but no sign at all of any men actually at work. They had left their tools, though. There was a wheelbarrow, a pile of steel girders, a cement mixer . . . even if we could have climbed over the fence it would have been hard to get through.

"We've got to go back!" I shouted.

But it was too late. Bastille and Lavache had already arrived at the entrance to the bridge and were moving more slowly, both of them smiling. They knew they had us trapped. Lavache had his knife out. It was difficult to hear with the noise of the traffic, but I think he was humming.

We couldn't go back. We couldn't climb the fence. If we jumped over the side, we'd probably drown. This was only March and the water would be ice-cold. Just sixty feet separated us from the two Frenchmen. There was nothing we could do.

And that was when I saw the boat. It was what they called a Bateau Mouche, one of those long, elegant boats with glass windows and ceilings that carry tourists up and down the river throughout the day and night. This one was full of people enjoying a dinner and dance. I heard the music drifting up to us. They were playing a waltz, the "Blue Danube." A strange choice considering they were on the Seine. Already the boat was slipping under the bridge. Another few seconds and it would have disappeared down toward the Eiffel Tower.

"Jump, Tim!" I ordered.

"Right, Nick!" Tim jumped up and down on the spot.

"No. I mean—jump off the bridge!"

"What?" Tim looked at me as if I were mad.

Bastille was only five steps away from us now. I ran to the edge of the bridge, hoisted myself up, and jumped. Tim did the same, a few seconds behind me. I caught a glimpse of Bastille, staring at us, his face twisted between anger and amazement. Then I was falling through space with the river, the bridge, and the boat corkscrewing around me. I thought

I might have mistimed it but then my feet hit something and I crashed onto the deck. I was lucky. I had hit the front of the boat, where there was a sheet of tarpaulin stretched out amid a tangle of ropes. It broke my fall.

Tim was less fortunate. He had jumped a few seconds after me, allowing the boat to travel a few feet farther forward. I heard the glass shatter as he went feetfirst through the glass roof. There were more screams and the music stopped. I pulled myself up and gazed groggily through a window. Tim had landed on one of the tables and was lying there, sprawled out, surrounded by broken plates and glasses and with what looked like a whole roast duck in his lap.

"Que fais-tu? Qu'est-ce qui se passe?"

A man in a blue uniform had appeared on the deck. He was staring at me in horror. It was the captain of the Bateau Mouche. There were a couple of waiters with him. I didn't even struggle as the three of them grabbed hold of me. I wondered if they were going to lock me up or throw me over the side. Certainly it didn't look as if they were going to invite me in for a dance and something to eat.

I twisted around and took one last look back at the bridge. Bastille and Lavache were leaning over the side, watching, and as I was dragged inside they vanished, swallowed up in the gathering gloom.

DOWN-AND-OUT

You won't meet many thirteen-year-olds who have been locked up in prisons on both sides of the Channel, but I'm one of them. I did time in Strangeday Hall, sharing a cell with Johnny Powers, England's public enemy number one,* and here I was in prison in Paris, this time with Tim. It was half past nine in the evening. We'd been given dinner—bread and water—but the fact that it was French bread and Perrier didn't make it taste any better.

Miraculously, neither Tim nor I had been hurt jumping from the bridge. The captain had locked us both up in the kitchen on board the ship, and by the time we docked, the police were already waiting. I suppose he must have radioed on ahead. I hadn't tried to argue as we were thrown into the back of a van and driven at high speed through the streets of Paris. Nobody spoke English and even if they had they wouldn't have believed us. I assumed they'd call the British consul or someone. I would leave the explanations until then.

Neither of us had said anything for a while but at last Tim broke the silence. "That's the last time I buy a Bestlé yogurt," he muttered.

"It wasn't their fault, Tim," I said, although I knew how he felt. We hadn't even been in Paris one day and we'd

*See *Public Enemy Number Two*

witnessed one murder, been chased by two killers, and were now locked up ourselves. It was probably just as well that we weren't planning to stay a whole week. "I just wish I knew what it was all about," I added.

"They tried to kill us, Nick," Tim explained. "They nearly *did* kill us!"

"I noticed, Tim. But why?"

Tim thought for a moment. "Perhaps they don't like foreigners?" he suggested.

"No. They were looking for something. Something they thought we had." I already knew it had to be tied in with Marc Chabrol, the steward we had met at the Gare du Nord, and the packet of sugar he had given us. But what could be so important about a packet of sugar? It was still in my back pocket. I reached in and took it out. "This is what they were after," I said.

"Sugar?"

"Unless there's something else inside . . ."

I was about to open it there and then but at that moment the door opened and a young policeman with close-cropped hair and glasses walked in. I slipped the sugar back into my pocket. I could always examine it later.

"This way, please," the policeman said.

He led us back out and down a corridor, then into an interrogation room that smelled of cigarette smoke. There was a table and three chairs but nothing else, not even a window. A naked lightbulb hung on a short cord from the ceiling. The policeman gestured and we all sat down.

"You are English," he said.

"That's right," I said. The man obviously had a first-class brain.

"This is an outrage!" Tim exclaimed. "You can't keep us here. I demand to speak to the British ambassador! If the British ambassador is busy, I'll speak to his wife."

The policeman leaned forward. "First of all, monsieur, I can keep you here for as long as I wish," he said. "And secondly, I doubt very much that the British ambassador would be interested in you. Or his wife!"

"Why wouldn't he be interested in his wife?" Tim asked.

The policeman ignored him. "You and your small brother have caused great damage to one of our Bateaux Mouches," he went on. "It is most fortunate that nobody was injured. I wish to know why the two of you jumped off the bridge. You were trying to commit suicide, perhaps? Or could it have been a joke?"

"It was no joke," I said. "There were two men trying to kill us . . ."

The policeman looked at me in disbelief.

"It's true," I went on. "They said their names were Bastille and Lavache. They had a knife . . ."

"Tell me your names," the policeman commanded. He took out a notebook and prepared to write.

"I'm Tim Diamond," Tim said. "You may have heard of me."

"No, monsieur . . ."

"Well, I'm a well-known detective back in London." Tim pointed at the notebook. "That's the capital of England," he added helpfully.

The policeman paused and took a deep breath. He was getting older by the minute. "I am aware of that," he said. "May I ask, what is your business here in Paris?"

"Of course you can ask!" Tim said.

The policeman groaned. "What is your business?" he demanded.

"We're on vacation," I told him. "We only arrived today. We're staying in Le Chat Gris in the Latin Quarter . . ."

The policeman looked at me strangely, as if he were seeing me properly for the first time. "Le Chat Gris . . ." he repeated. He closed the notebook. "Could you please wait here for a minute."

He stood up and left the room.

In fact it was ten minutes before he returned. The moment he walked in, I noticed there was something different about him. He was brisk, emotionless. And when he spoke, he did his best not to meet our eyes. "I have spoken with my superior officer," he said. "And he says that you are free to go!"

"How can we be free to go when we're locked up in here?" Tim asked.

"No, no, no, monsieur. He says that you may leave."

"They're unlocking the door and letting us out," I explained.

"As far as we are concerned, this incident is closed." The policeman did the same to his notebook.

"What about Bastille and Lavache?" I asked.

"We have no record of these men. It is our view that they do not exist!"

"What?"

"You jump off the bridge for a joke or maybe as a game and you make up the story of the killers to explain your actions. That is the view of my superintendent."

"Well, he can't be as super as all that," I growled.

But there was no point arguing. For whatever their reasons, the French police had decided to let us go. As far as I was concerned, I just wanted to get out of jail. And out of Paris, too, for that matter. I'd only been there for a day but so far our visit had been less fun than a French lesson—and twice as dangerous.

"Let's go, Tim," I said.

It was almost eleven o'clock by the time we got back to the Latin Quarter, but the night wasn't over yet. Tim wanted to stop for a beer and I was still anxious to open the packet of sugar that was burning a hole in my back pocket. We looked for a café and quite by coincidence found ourselves outside an old-fashioned, artistic sort of place whose name I knew. It was La Palette, the very same café where the train steward, Marc Chabrol, had asked us to meet.

He wasn't there, of course. Right now, if Chabrol was

sipping coffee, it was with two wings and a halo. But there was someone there that we recognized. He was sitting out in the front, smoking a cigar, gazing into the night sky. There was no way I'd forget the hat. It was Jed Mathis, the businessman we had met on the train.

Tim saw him. "It's Ned," he said.

"You mean Jed," I said.

"Why don't we join him?"

"Forget it!" I grabbed Tim and we walked forward, continuing toward our hotel.

"But, Nick! He paid for the drinks on the train. Maybe he'd buy me a beer."

"Yes, Tim. But think for a minute. What's he doing at La Palette?" I looked at my watch. It was eleven o'clock exactly. "It could just be a coincidence. But maybe he's waiting for someone. Maybe he's waiting for us! Don't you remember what Marc Chabrol said?"

"He asked us if we wanted to buy a Kit Kat."

"Yes. But after that. In the station, he warned us about someone who he called 'the mad American.' Jed Mathis is American! He said he was from Texas."

"You think Mathis killed Chabrol?"

"Mathis was on the train. And Chabrol ended up underneath it. I don't know. But I don't think we should hang around and have drinks with him. I think we should go home!"

We hurried on. Le Chat Gris loomed up ahead of us, but before we got there I noticed something else.

There was a man standing opposite the hotel. It was hard to recognize him because he was holding a camera up to his face, taking a picture. I heard the click of the button and the whir as the film wound on automatically. He wasn't a tourist. That much was certain. Not unless his idea of a vacation shot was two English tourists about to check out. Because the photograph he had taken had been of us. There could be no doubt about it. I could feel the telephoto lens halfway up my nose.

He lowered the camera and now I recognized the man. He had been standing in the reception area that morning when we left: a dark-haired man in a gray suit.

Marc Chabrol, the steward.

Bastille and Lavache.

And now this.

Just what was happening in Paris and why did it all have to happen to us?

A car suddenly drew up, a blue Citroën. The man with the camera got in and a moment later they were roaring past us. I just caught a glimpse of the driver, smoking a cigarette with one hand, steering with the other. Then they were gone.

Tim had already walked into the hotel. Feeling increasingly uneasy, I followed him in.

We took the key from the squinting receptionist and took the stairs back to the top of the hotel. There were a lot of them and the stairway was so narrow that the walls brushed both my shoulders as I climbed. Finally we got to the last floor. Tim stopped for breath. Then he unlocked our door.

Our room had been torn apart. The sheets had been pulled off the bed and the mattress slashed open, springs and enough hair to cover a horse tumbling out onto the floor. Every drawer had been opened, overturned, and smashed. The carpet had been pulled up and the curtains down. Tim's jackets and pants had been scattered all over the room. And I mean scattered. We found one arm on a windowsill, one leg in the shower, a single pocket under what was left of the bed. Our suitcases had been cut open and turned inside out. We'd need another suitcase just to carry the old ones down to the trash.

Tim gazed at the destruction. "I can't say I think too much of room service, Nick," he said.

"This isn't room service, Tim!" I exploded. "The room's been searched!"

"What do you think they were looking for?"

"This!" I took out the packet of sugar. Once again I was tempted to open it—but this wasn't the right time. "This is the only thing Chabrol gave us back at the station. It must be the object that Bastille was talking about." I slid it back into my pocket, then thought again. It seemed that Bastille was determined to get his hands on the sugar. I wouldn't be safe carrying it. It was better to leave it in the hotel room. After all, they'd already searched the place once. It was unlikely they'd think of coming back.

I looked around, then slid the sugar into the roll of toilet paper in the bathroom, inside the cardboard tube. Nobody would notice it there and the police could pick it up later. Because that was the next step.

"We've got to call the police," I said.

"We've just come from the police," Tim reminded me.

"I know. But if they see our room, they've got to believe us. And as soon as they're here, I'll show them the packet. Maybe they'll be able to work the whole thing out."

I looked for the telephone and eventually found it—or what was left of it. You'd have to be an expert at electronics or at least very good at jigsaws to use it again.

"Why don't we talk to the man downstairs?" Tim asked.

I thought of the squinting receptionist. Only that morning he'd been talking to the man in the gray suit, the one who'd just taken our photograph.

"I don't trust him," I said. At that moment I wouldn't have trusted my own mother.

Tim held up a short-sleeved shirt. It had been a long-sleeved shirt when he had packed it. He looked as if he was going to burst into tears. At least he could use the rest of the shirt as a handkerchief if he did.

"Let's go back down, Tim," I said. "We can call the police from the lobby. I noticed a phone booth."

"What's the French for 911?" Tim asked.

"Seventeen," I replied. I'd seen it written next to the phone.

But the phone in the hotel was out of order. There was a sign on the window reading *"Hors de service."* I translated for Tim and he went over to the receptionist. "We want to call the police," he said.

"Please?" The receptionist narrowed his eye. I think he would have liked to have narrowed both his eyes, but the one on the left wasn't working.

"No," Tim explained. "Police." He saluted and bent his knees, doing an imitation of a policeman. The receptionist stared at him as if he had gone mad.

"*Les flics*," I said.

"Ah!" The receptionist nodded. Then he leaned forward and pointed. "You go out the door. You turn left. Then you take the first turning left again," he growled. He actually spoke pretty good English even if the words had trouble getting past his throat. "There's a police station just at the next corner."

We left the hotel, turned left, and then immediately left again. We found ourselves in a narrow alleyway that twisted its way through the shadows before coming to a brick wall.

"This is wrong," I said.

"You don't want to go to the police anymore?" Tim asked.

"No, Tim. I still want to go to the police but this is the wrong way. It's a dead end."

"Maybe we have to climb over the wall."

"I don't think so . . ."

I was getting worried. After everything that had happened to us so far, the last place I wanted to be was a dead end . . .

or anywhere else with the word *dead* in it. And I was right. There was a sudden squeal as a van appeared racing toward us. The squeal, incidentally, came from Tim. The van was reversing. For a moment I thought it was going to crush us, but it stopped, just inches away. The back doors flew open. Two men got out.

Everything was happening too quickly. I couldn't even tell who the men were or if I had seen them before. I saw one of them lash out and Tim spun around, crumpling to the ground. Then it was my turn. Something hard hit me on the back of the head. My legs buckled. I fell forward and one of the men must have caught me as I felt myself being half-pushed, half-carried into the back of the van.

Tim was next to me. "Some vacation!" he said.

Then either they hit me again or they hit him. Or maybe they hit both of us. Either way, I was out cold.

PARIS BY NIGHT

I knew I was in trouble before I even opened my eyes. For a
start, I was sitting up. If everything that had happened up
until now had been a horrible dream—which it should have
been—I would be lying in my nice warm bed in London
with the kettle whistling in the kitchen and maybe Tim doing
the same in the bath. But not only was I sitting in a hard,
wooden chair, my feet were tied together with something
that felt suspiciously like packing tape and my hands were
similarly bound behind my back. When I did finally open my
eyes, it only got worse. Tim was next to me looking pale and
confused . . . by which I mean even more confused than
usual. And Bastille and Lavache were sitting opposite us,
both of them smoking.

The four of us were in a large, empty room that might
once have been the dining room of a grand château but was
now empty and dilapidated. The floor was wooden and the
walls white plaster, with no pictures or decorations. A
broken chandelier hung from the ceiling. In fact quite a lot
of the ceiling was hanging from the ceiling. Half of it seemed
to be peeling off.

I had no idea how much time had passed since they'd
knocked us out and bundled us into the back of a delivery

van. An hour? A week? I couldn't see my watch—it was pinned somewhere behind me, along with the wrist it was on—so I twisted around and looked out of the window. The glass was so dust-covered that I could barely see outside, but from the light I would have said it was early evening. If so, we had been unconscious for about fifteen hours! I wondered where we were. Somewhere in the distance I thought I heard singing, the sound of a choir. But the music was foreign—and not French. It sounded vaguely religious, which made me think of churches. And that made me think of funerals. I just hoped they weren't singing for us.

"Good evening," Bastille muttered. He hadn't changed out of the dirty linen suit he had been wearing when we met him the day before. It was so crumpled now that I wondered if he had slept in it.

"What time is it?" Tim asked.

"It is time for you to talk!" Bastille blew a cloud of smoke into Tim's face.

Tim coughed. "You know those things can damage your health!" he remarked.

Not quickly enough, I thought. But I said nothing.

"It is *your* health that should concern you, my friend," Bastille replied.

"I'm perfectly well, thank you," Tim said.

"I mean—your health if you fail to tell us what we want to know!" Bastille's green eyes flared. He was even uglier when he was angry. "You have put us to a great deal of trouble," he went on. "We've searched you and this morning we searched your room. Are you going to tell us where it is?"

"It's on the top floor of the hotel!" Tim exclaimed.

"Not the room!" Bastille swore and choked on his cigarette. "I am talking about the packet that you were given by Marc Chabrol."

"The ex-steward," Lavache added. He giggled, and, looking at his apelike hands, I suddenly knew how Chabrol had managed to "fall" under a train.

I'd said nothing throughout all this. I was just glad that I'd decided not to bring the packet with us. The two men must have searched Tim and me while we were unconscious. They had found nothing and it looked like they weren't going to go back and search the hotel room a second time.

"He gave us a cup of coffee," Tim was saying. "But we drank it. Unless you're talking about . . . wait a minute—"

"Who *are* you people?" I cut in. I didn't want him to say any more. So long as we had the packet, they wouldn't kill us. They needed to know where it was. But the moment they heard it was hidden in the toilet, we were dead. That much was certain. I would just have to keep them talking and hope for the best. "Look . . ." I went on. "The steward didn't give us anything. We're just here on vacation."

"*Non, non, non!*" Bastille shook his head. "Do not try lying to me, *mon petit ami*. I know that your brother is a private detective. I also know that he was sent to Paris by Interpol. I know that he is working on a special assigment."

His face turned ugly, which, with his face, wasn't difficult. "Now I want you to tell me how much you know and who gave you your information."

"But I don't know anything!" Tim wailed.

He'd never spoken a truer word in his life. Tim knew nothing about any special assignment. He'd have had trouble telling anyone his own shoe size. And he also hadn't realized that this was all his fault. If only he'd kept his mouth shut on the train! He'd told Jed Mathis and the old woman that he was working for Interpol. Could one of them have passed it on? Jed Mathis . . . ?

Beware the mad American . . .

It was too late to worry about that. I realized that Tim was still talking. He had told them everything. The competition on the yogurt container. The free weekend. The truth.

"He's right," I admitted. "We're just tourists. We're not working for anyone."

"It was a strawberry yogurt!" Tim burbled. "Bestlé yogurts. They're only eighty calories each . . ."

"We don't know anything!" I said.

Bastille and Lavache moved closer to each other and began to mutter in low, dark voices. I couldn't understand a word they were saying, but somehow I didn't like the sound of it. I tried to break free from the chair but it was useless. Things weren't looking good. By now they must have realized that they were wrong about us, that we were exactly what we said. But they weren't just going to order us a taxi and pretend the whole thing had never happened. As they're always saying in the old movies . . . we knew too much. I still had no idea who they were or what they were doing, but we knew their names and had seen their faces. That was enough.

The two men straightened up. "We have decided that we believe you," Bastille said.

"That's terrific!" Tim exclaimed.

"So now we are going to kill you."

"Oh!" His face fell.

Lavache walked to the far side of the room and I strained my neck to watch him. He reached out with both hands and suddenly a whole section of the wall slid to one side. I realized now that it wasn't a wall at all but a set of floor-to-ceiling doors. There was another room on the other side, filled with activity, and at that moment I realized what this was all about. Perhaps I should have guessed from the start.

Drugs.

The other room was a laboratory. I could see metal tables piled high with white powder. More white powder being weighed on complicated electronic scales. White powder being spooned into plastic bags. There were about half a dozen people working there, young men and women with dirty faces but pristine laboratory coats. They were handling the white powder in complete silence, as if they knew that it was death they were carrying in their hands and that if it heard them it would somehow find them out.

Lavache lumbered into the room, vanishing from sight. When he reappeared, he was holding something that he handed to Bastille. Right then I was more scared than I've ever been in my life, and you know me . . . I don't scare easily. But suddenly I remembered that I was thirteen years old, that I hadn't started shaving yet, and that my mother (who'd been shaving for years) was thousands of miles away. I was so scared I almost wanted to cry.

Bastille was holding a bottle of pills.

He approached Tim first. "These are superstrength," he said. "I think five of them will be enough."

"No, thank you," Tim said. "I haven't got a headache."

"They're not headache pills, Tim," I said.

Bastille grabbed hold of Tim and forced his mouth open. He had counted five pills into the palm of his hand and I watched, powerless, as he forced them down Tim's throat. Then he turned and began to walk toward me.

"They don't taste very nice!" I heard Tim say, but I'd gone crazy, rocking back and forth, yelling, kicking with my feet, trying to tear apart the packing tape around my wrists. It was useless. I felt Lavache grab hold of my shoulders while at the same time Bastille took hold of my chin. I don't know what was worse. Feeling his bony fingers against my face or knowing there was nothing I could do as he forced my mouth open. His right hand came up and the next moment there were four or five pills on my tongue. They had an evil taste. I drew a breath, meaning to spit them out, but his hand was already over my mouth, almost suffocating me. I screamed silently and felt the pills trickle down the back of my throat. I almost felt them drop into the pit of my stomach. Then Bastille pulled his hand clear and my head sank forward. I said nothing. I thought I was dead. I thought he had killed me.

Things happened very quickly after that. It seemed to me that the lights in the room had brightened and that somebody had turned up the heat. My eyes hurt. And then the walls began to revolve, slowly at first, like the start of a ride at an amusement park. But there was nothing fun about this. Drugs are poison and I was sure I had just been given a lethal overdose. I was sweating. I tried to speak but my tongue refused to move; anyway, my mouth was too dry.

I heard the packing tape being ripped off and felt my hands come free. Lavache was standing behind me. I tried to look at him, but my head lolled uselessly. He pulled me off the chair and carried me outside. Bastille followed with Tim.

There was a white van waiting for us in an enclosed courtyard—we could have been anywhere. I looked back at the house we had just left. It was a gray building, three stories high. Most of its paint had flaked off and there were scorch marks, as if it had been involved in a fire. About half the windows were shattered. Others had been bricked in. The place looked derelict. I guessed it was supposed to.

I was bundled into the van and the next moment the

engine started up, roaring at me like a mechanical beast. I almost expected it to come bursting through the floor, to gobble me up. The noise hammered at my ears and I groaned. Tim was thrown in next to me. The doors slammed. My stomach heaved. We were off.

There was a small window set in the door and I managed to stagger over to it and pull myself onto my knees to look out. But it was hard to see anything. The world was spinning faster now, tilting from side to side. I just made out a series of letters in red neon, but it seemed to take me forever to work out the three words they formed:

THE FRENCH CONFECTION

The van turned a corner and I lost my balance. Before I fell, I caught a glimpse of a blue star . . . on a flag or perhaps on the side of a building. Then the sound of the van's engine rose up again and swallowed me. The floor hit me in the face. Or maybe it was me who had hit the floor. I no longer knew the difference.

The journey took an hour . . . a month . . . a year. I had no idea. What was the stuff they had given me? Whatever it was, it was taking over, killing me. I could feel it happening, an inch at a time. The van stopped. Hands that no longer belonged to bodies pulled us out. Then the sidewalk slapped me in the face, there was another scream from the engine, and suddenly I knew that we were alone.

"Tim . . . ?" I gasped the word. But Tim was no longer there. He had turned into some horrible animal with sixteen eyes, tentacles, and . . .

I forced myself to concentrate, knowing that it was the drug that was doing it to me. The image dissolved and there he was again. My brother.

"Nick . . ." He staggered to his feet. All three of them. Things weren't back to normal yet.

The sky changed from red to blue to yellow to green. I stood up as well.

"Must get help," I said.

Tim groaned.

We were back in the center of Paris. It was late at night. And Paris had never looked like this before.

There was the Seine but the water had gone, replaced by red wine that glowed darkly in the moonlight. It was twisting its way underneath the bridges, but now that I looked more closely, I saw that they had changed, too. They had become huge sticks of French bread. There was a sudden buzzing. A Bateau Mouche had suddenly sprouted huge blue wings and legs. It leaped out of the water and onto one of the bridges, tearing a great chunk out with a hideous, hairy mouth before spiraling away into the night.

The ground underneath my feet had gone soft and I realized I was sinking into it. With a cry I lifted one foot and saw that the tar had melted and was dripping off my sneaker. Except the tar was yellow, not black.

"It's cheese!" I shouted. And it was. The entire street had turned into cheese—soft, ripe, French cheese. I gasped for air, choking on the smell. At the same time, the cheese pulled me into it. Another few seconds and I would be sucked underneath the surface.

"Nick!" Tim called out.

And then the cheese was gone as he pointed with an arm that was now a mile long. There was a snail coming down the boulevard. No . . . not one snail but a thousand of them, each one the size of a house, slithering along ahead of the traffic, leaving a gray, slimy trail behind them. At one corner, the traffic lights had gone red and all the snails were squeaking at one another, a fantastic traffic jam of snails. At the same time, I heard what sounded like a gigantic burp and a frog, the size of a bus, bounded across my vision, leaping over a building. But the frog was missing its legs. It was supporting itself on giant crutches.

The world twisted, heaved, broke up, and then re-formed with all the pieces in different positions: a jigsaw puzzle in the hands of a destructive child.

Suddenly we were surrounded by grinning stone figures, jabbering and staring at us with empty stone eyes. I recognized them: the gargoyles from Notre Dame. There must have been a hundred of them. One of them was sitting on Tim's shoulder like a gray chimpanzee. But Tim didn't seem to have noticed it.

Light. Car lights. Everywhere. A horn sounded. I had

stepped into the road—but it didn't matter because the cars were the size of matchboxes. They were all Citroëns. Every one of them. And they were being followed by cyclists. The Tour de France had come early. All the cyclists were smoking cigarettes.

Tim was clutching a streetlamp. Now he was wearing a striped jersey and a beret and there was a string of onions hanging from his side. "*Je suis*," he said. "*Tu es, il est . . .*"

I opened my mouth to reply.

Crash! Crash! Crash!

I saw it before he did. Perhaps he didn't see it at all. Even now, with the drug pumping through my body, I knew that it wasn't real, that I was hallucinating. But it made no difference. As far as I was concerned, everything I saw was real. And if it was real, it could kill me. It could step on me. It could crush me.

The Eiffel Tower! On our first day in Paris we had crossed the city to visit it. Now the Eiffel Tower was coming to visit us. There it was, walking across Paris, swinging one iron foot, then the next, moving like some sort of giant, four-legged crab. One of its feet came down in a pancake stall. Wood shattered. Pancakes flew in all directions. Somebody screamed.

The cheese was getting softer. I was sinking into a boulevard of Brie, a two-lane highway of Camembert. The squirming yellow slipped around my waist, rose over my shoulder, and twisted around my neck. I didn't even try to fight. I'd had enough. I waited for it to pull me under.

I thought I was going to die and if I'd waited another minute I might well have. But just then I heard what I thought was an owl, hooting in my ear. At the same time I found myself staring at a face I knew. A dark-haired man in a gray-colored suit. I became aware of a blue flashing light that either belonged to a dragon or a police car. I looked up and saw something driving out of the moon, flying through the sky toward me. An ambulance.

"Don't go to sleep!" a voice commanded. "Don't go to sleep! Don't go to sleep!"

But it was too late. I went to sleep.

Forever.

THE MAD AMERICAN

"You're lucky to be alive," the man said.

It was two days later. I don't want to tell you about those two days. I'd spent both of them in a hospital in Paris and all I can say is, if you've ever had your stomach pumped, you'll know there are plenty of things you can do that are more fun. I don't remember much about the first day. The next day, I felt like a washing machine that's been left on too long. All I'd eaten in the entire time was a little bread and water. Fortunately, the water didn't have bubbles. I don't think I could have managed the bubbles.

And now, here I was in the headquarters of Sûreté, the French police force. It's funny how police stations are the same the whole world over. This may have been grander and spiffier than New Scotland Yard. The curtains were velvet and the pictures on the wall showed some gray-haired Frenchman in a suit rather than our own gray-haired Queen in a crown. But it still smelled the same.

Tim was sitting next to me. He was the color of the yogurt that had brought us here in the first place, with eyes like crushed strawberries. His hair was disheveled and he looked like he hadn't slept in a month. I was going to say something but decided against it. I probably looked just as bad.

We were in the office of the chief of police—a man called Christien Moire. I knew because I'd seen the name and title on the door. It was on his desk, too. Maybe he was worried he was going to forget it. He was the man in the gray suit whom I'd seen standing outside Le Chat Gris, the man who had been talking to the receptionist and who had later taken our photograph. Things were beginning to add up even if I still had no idea of the total.

"Another one hour and it would have been too late," Moire went on. He spoke English as if he had no idea what he was saying, lingering on every word. He had the sort of accent you get in bad television shows: *Anuzzer wan our an' eet would 'ave bin too late.* I hope you get the idea. "You were very lucky," he added.

"Sure," I muttered. "And we'd have been even luckier if you'd arrived a couple of hours before."

Moire shrugged. "I'm sorry," he said. But his dark, empty eyes looked about as apologetic as two lumps of ice. "We had no idea you had been taken," he went on.

"Who are you?" Tim demanded. "You call yourself the Sûreté. But what exactly are you sure about?"

"The Sûreté," Moire repeated, "is the French police force. I am the head of a special unit fighting the traffic in . . ."

". . . drugs." I completed the sentence.

"*Exactement.* I have to say that you and your brother seem to have turned up in the wrong place at the wrong time. If I hadn't been watching you . . ."

"You were at the hotel," I said. "I saw you outside. You had a camera . . ."

"Is that your hobby?" Tim asked. "Photography?"

Christien Moire stared at Tim through narrow eyes. He obviously hadn't ever met anyone like him before. "Le Chat Gris has been under surveillance," he said. "Perhaps I should explain . . ."

"Perhaps you should," I said.

Moire lit a Gauloise. It's a funny thing about the French. Not only do they all smoke, but they smoke the most horrible cigarettes in the world. Forget about the health warning on the pack. The smoke from Moire's cigarette was so thick, you could have printed it on that.

"For some time now," he began, "we have been aware of a drug-smuggling operation. Somebody has been moving drugs to London . . . using the trains under the Channel. We still don't know how they're doing it. We have searched the trains from top to bottom but we have found nothing. Worse still, we do not know who they are."

"Is there anything you *do* know?" I asked.

Moire glanced at me with unfriendly eyes. "We know only the code name of the man behind the operation," he replied.

"The Mad American," I said.

That surprised Moire, but he tried not to show it. "The drugs arrive from Marseille," he went on. "They are weighed and packaged somewhere in Paris. Then the Mad American arranges for them to be sent to London. We've been working with the English police to try to stop them. So far we have had no success in London. But in Paris we had one lucky break."

"Le Chat Gris," I said.

"Yes, we learned that the hotel is sometimes used by the Mad American. When dealers arrive from London to buy his drugs, that is where they stay. He meets them there. They pay him the money and then his two associates—Jacques Bastille and Luc Lavache—arrange for the drugs to be sent on the train."

"So *that's* why you photographed us!" I said. "You thought we'd come to Paris to buy drugs!"

"I know it sounds unlikely," Moire said. "An English kid and his idiotic brother—"

"Nick isn't idiotic!" Tim protested.

"We became interested in you the moment you reported that Bastille and Lavache had attempted to kill you," Moire went on. "I ordered the photograph to be taken so that we could check you against our criminal files."

"But if you thought we were criminals, why did you let us go in the first place?" I asked. It had puzzled me at the time, the policeman suddenly changing his mind and telling us we could leave.

"The answer to that is simple," Moire said. "We still had no idea what part you had to play in all this, but you had mentioned Le Chat Gris and that was enough. It was important that the Mad American should not be aware that the police were involved. I personally ordered your release, and at the same time I made sure that we kept you under—how do you say?—surveillance. This was very lucky for you, considering how things turned out."

"You were following us."

"Yes. I saw you go back to the hotel, and minutes later I saw the van with the two men who knocked you out and kidnapped you. We followed the van but unfortunately lost it in traffic . . ."

". . . so you don't know where we were taken."

"No. But I knew that you were in danger and I had every policeman in Paris looking out for you. One of them saw you and radioed HQ. By that time they had pumped you with enough drugs to kill a horse."

"Why would they want to kill a horse?" Tim asked.

Moire ignored him. "We only got to you in the nick of time. Another ten minutes, and the two of you would now be in Père Lachaise."

"You mean, another hotel," Tim said.

"No. Père Lachaise is a cemetery."

"Okay. You saved us, Monsieur Moire," I said. "But now, if you don't mind, I'm heading back to the hotel, packing, and leaving for London."

"That's right, Monsieur Loire," Tim agreed. "We're out of here!"

"I'm afraid not." Moire hadn't raised his voice. If anything, he had done the exact opposite. But that's the thing about the French. When they're being really nasty, they don't shout. They whisper. "You realize that I could have you arrested?" he asked.

I almost laughed. "What for?" I demanded.

"You were found in the middle of Paris, full of drugs," the police chief explained. He sounded almost reasonable. "Two English tourists who decided to experiment with these forbidden substances . . ."

"That's a complete lie!" I exclaimed.

"Yes!" Tim agreed. "We're not tourists!"

"And then there is the matter of the Bateau Mouche . . ." Moire continued. "You jumped off a bridge, endangering the lives of the people on the boat. This could also prove to be drug-related."

"What do you want, Moire?" I demanded.

Moire leaned forward. His face could have been carved out of stone. Even the cigarette smoke seemed to have solidified. "There are two things we wish to find out," he said. "First, who is the Mad American?"

"Why don't you ask Bastille and Lavache?" I demanded.

"They wouldn't tell us anything. And if we did arrest them, it would only let their boss know that we were getting close . . . and that would ruin everything. The second thing we wish to know is, how are they smuggling the drugs across the Channel? As I have told you, we have searched the train many times . . . but with no success. These packets of white powder—they must be somewhere. But . . ." He smacked his forehead with the palm of his hand. "It is infuriating!"

"What do you want us to do?" I asked.

"I want you to go back to the hotel," Moire replied. "It will be as if nothing has happened."

"Why?"

"Because you can be useful to me . . . on the inside. My men will continue to watch you. You'll be completely safe. But maybe you can find the answers to the questions. And if there is anything to report . . ."

"Forget it!" I snapped.

"Right!" Tim nodded. "Bestlé only paid for four days. We can't possibly afford it."

"Bestlé?" For the first time Moire looked puzzled. "Who is Bestlé?"

"It doesn't matter," I replied. "We're British citizens. You can't blackmail us!"

"You don't think so?" Moire almost smiled. "You are Europeans now, my friend. And if you don't do exactly as I tell you, let me assure you that you will be spending a great deal of time inside a European jail."

I wanted to argue, but I could see there was no point. The last person to argue with Christien Moire probably found himself with a one-way ticket to Devil's Island.

He knew he'd beaten me. "Go back to Le Chat Gris and wait for further instructions," he said. "Don't worry about the bill. I will see to it."

"And what if we get killed?" I asked.

"My department will pay for the funeral, too."

I sank back in my chair. There was nothing I could say. Not in French. Not in English. It really wasn't fair.

And that was how we found ourselves, a few hours later, back in our room at Le Chat Gris. As I'd walked back into the hotel, I'd known how those French aristocrats must have felt as they took their last steps toward the guillotine. The receptionist had almost fallen off his chair when he saw us and he'd been on the telephone before we'd reached the elevator. The Mad American would have presumed we were dead. Now he'd know he was wrong. How long would it take him to correct his mistake?

Tim sat down on the bed. He was actually looking quite cheerful, which made me feel even worse. "Maybe this isn't so bad, Nick," he said.

"Tim!" I cried. "How bad can it get?"

"We're working for the French police now," he said. "This could be good for business! *Tim Diamond Inc.* . . . *London and Paris*. That'll look good on the door."

"It'll look even better on your gravestone," I said. "Don't you understand, Tim?" We're not working for anyone! Christien Moire was lying through his teeth!"

"You mean . . . he isn't a policeman?"

"Of course he's a policeman. But he doesn't want us to work for him. He's using us!" I'd taken a guidebook of Paris out of my suitcase. Now I sat down next to Tim. "Moire wants to find out the identity of the Mad American," I explained. "What's the best way to do that?"

"Just ask for Tim Diamond . . ."

"Just *use* Tim Diamond. He's sent us back here because he knows that our turning up again will panic the Mad American. He's already tried to kill us twice. He's certain to try again—and this time Moire will be watching. He's using us as bait in a trap, Tim. The Mad American kills us. Moire gets the Mad American. It's as simple as that."

I opened the guidebook. "I'm not sitting here, waiting to be shot," I said.

"Where do you want to be shot?" Tim asked.

"I don't want to be shot anywhere! That's why I'm going to find the Mad American before he finds us." I started to thumb through the pages. I still didn't know what I was looking for, but I had a good idea. "After we were knocked out, we were taken to the Mad American's headquarters," I said.

"But we were knocked out!" Tim said. "We didn't see anything."

"We didn't see much," I agreed. "But there were some clues. A blue star. Some words in a shop window—THE FRENCH CONFECTION. And when we were tied up, I heard something. Music. Singing."

"Do you think that was the Mad American?"

"No, Tim. It was coming from a building nearby." I

stopped, trying to remember what I had heard. "It wasn't French singing," I said. "It was different . . . It was foreign."

Sitting next to me on the bed, Tim was making a strange noise. I thought for a moment that he had a stomachache. Then I realized he was trying to hum the tune.

"That's right, Tim," I said. "It was something like that. Only a bit more human."

Tim stopped. I tried to think. How had the singing gone? It had been sad and somehow dislocated. A choir and a single male voice. At times it had been more like wailing than singing. Remembering it now made me think of a church. Was that it? Had it been religious music? But if so, what religion?

I'm not sure what happened first. The thought seemed to come into my mind at exactly the same moment as I found myself looking at the words *The Jewish Quarter* in the guidebook in my hands.

"Jewish music!" I exclaimed.

"Jewish?"

"The music that we heard, Tim. It was coming from a synagogue!"

Tim's eyes lit up. "You think we were taken to Jerusalem?"

"No, Tim. We were in Paris. But there's an area of Paris that's full of synagogues." I waved the book at him. "Le Marais. That's what it's called. The Jewish section of Paris . . ."

"But how big is it?" Tim asked.

I read the page in front of me:

Originally a swamp, the Marais has grown to become one of the most fashionable areas of Paris. Its narrow streets are filled with shops and boutiques including some of the city's most elegant cafés and cake shops. The Marais is home to the Jewish Quarter with numerous synagogues and kosher restaurants based around the Rue des Rosiers.

There was a map showing the area. It had only a couple of dozen roads. "It doesn't look too big," I said. "And at least we know what we're looking for. The French Confection."

"But what *is* The French Confection, Nick?"

"I think it must be a shop. Maybe it sells cakes or candy or something. But once we've found it, we'll know we're right next to the factory. Find the sign and we'll have found the Mad American."

"And then?"

"Then we call Moire."

We slipped out of Le Chat Gris down the fire escape, dodging past Moire's men who were waiting for us at the front of the hotel. Then we dived into the nearest metro station and headed north.

It was a short walk from the station to the start of Le Marais—the Place Vendôme, one of those Paris squares where even the trees manage to look expensive. From there we headed down toward a big, elegant building that turned out to be the Picasso museum. I'd studied Picasso at school. He's the guy who painted women with eyes in the sides of their necks and tables with legs going the wrong way. It's called surrealism. Maybe I should have taken Tim in, as he's pretty surreal himself. But we didn't have time.

We backtracked and found ourselves in a series of long, narrow streets with buildings rising five stories on both sides. But I knew we were on the right track. There was no singing, but here and there I saw blue stars—the same stars I had glimpsed as I was bundled into the van. I knew what it was now: the six-pointed Star of David. There was one in every kosher food store and restaurant in the area.

We'd been following the Rue des Rosiers—the one I'd read about in the guidebook—but with no sign of the building where we'd been held. So now we started snaking up and down, taking the first on the right and the next on the left and so on. It was a pretty enough part of Paris, I'll say that for it. Tim had even forgotten our mission and stopped once or twice to take photographs. We'd been chased and threatened at knifepoint. We'd been kidnapped, drugged, and threatened again—this time by the French police. And he *still* thought we were on vacation!

And then, suddenly, we were there.

It was on one of the main streets of the area—the Rue de Sévigné. I recognized it at once: the burned face of the building, the broken windows, the ugly smokestacks . . . And there was the archway that we had driven through. There was a courtyard on the other side that was where the white van had been parked. I stood there in the sunlight, with people strolling past on the sidewalks, some carrying shopping bags, others pushing strollers. And none of them knew. The biggest drug factory in Paris was right in front of them, just sitting there between a café and a cake shop, right in the middle of the Marais. I couldn't believe I had found it so easily. It was hard to believe it was there at all.

"Nick . . . !" Tim whispered.

I grabbed hold of him and pulled him down behind a parked car as Bastille and Lavache appeared, coming out of the front door and walking across the courtyard. Each of them had a heavy box. Another shipment on its way out! It made me angry that anyone should be dumb enough to want to buy drugs and angrier still that these two grim reapers would be getting richer by selling them.

"What do we do now?" Tim whispered.

"Now we call Moire," I said.

"Right!" Tim straightened up. "Let's ask in there!"

Before I could stop him he had walked across the sidewalk and into the cake shop. There was the sign in the window that I had seen from the van. THE FRENCH CONFECTION. Why did the name bother me? Why did I feel it was connected with something or someone I had seen? It was too late to worry about it now. Tim was already inside. I followed him in.

I found myself in a long, narrow shop with a counter running down one wall. Everywhere I looked there were cakes and croissants, bowls of colored almonds and tiny pots of jam. The very air smelled of sugar and flour. On the counter stood one of the tallest wedding cakes I had ever seen: six platforms of swirly white icing with a marzipan bride and groom looking airsick up on the top. There was a bead curtain at the back and now it rattled as the owner of the shop passed through, coming out to serve us. And of course I knew her. I'd met her on the train.

Erica Nice.

She stopped behind the counter, obviously as surprised to see us as we were to see her.

"You . . . !" she began.

"Mrs. Nice!" Tim gurgled. I wondered how he had managed to remember her name. "We need to use your telephone. To call the police."

"I don't think so, Tim," I said.

Even as I spoke I was heading back toward the door. But I was already too late. Erica's hand came up and this time it wasn't holding an almond slice. It was the biggest gun I'd ever seen. Bigger than the wrinkled hand that held it. Its muzzle was as ugly as the smile on the old woman's face.

"But . . . but . . . but . . ." Tim stared.

"Erica Nice," I said. "I suppose I should have guessed. Madame Erica Nice. Say it fast and what do you get?"

"Madamericanice?" Tim suggested.

"Mad American," I said. "She's the one behind the drug racket, Tim. When we met her, she must have been checking the route. That's why she was on the train. And that's how Bastille and Lavache knew we were in Paris."

Erica Nice snarled at us. "Yes," she said. "I have to travel on the train now and then to keep an eye on things. Like that idiot steward—Marc Chabrol. He was scared. And scared people are no use to me."

"So you pushed him under a train," I said.

She shrugged. "I would have preferred to stab him. I did have my knitting needles, but unfortunately I was halfway through a wool sweater. Pushing was easier."

"And what now?" I asked. I wondered if she was going to shoot us herself or call her two thugs to finish the job for her. At the same time, I took a step forward, edging my way toward the counter and the giant wedding cake.

"Those idiots—Jacques and Luc—should have gotten rid of you when they had the chance," Erica hissed. "This time they will make no mistakes."

She turned to press a switch set in the wall. Presumably it connected the shop with the factory next door.

I leaped forward and threw my entire weight against the cake.

Erica half-turned. The gun came up.

The door of the shop burst open, the glass smashing.

And as Erica Nice gave a single shrill scream and disappeared beneath about twenty pounds of wedding cake,

Christien Moire and a dozen policemen hurled themselves into the shop. At the same time, I heard the blare of sirens as police cars swerved into the road from all directions.

I turned to Moire. "You followed us here?"

Moire nodded. "Of course. I had men on all sides of the hotel."

Erica Nice groaned and tried to fight her way out of several layers of sponge cake, jam, and butter cream. Tim leaned forward and scooped up a fragment of white icing. He popped it into his mouth.

"Nice cake," he said.

THE WHITE CLIFFS

The next day, Christien Moire drove us up to Calais and personally escorted us onto the ferry. It would have been easier to take the train, of course. But somehow Tim and I had had enough of trains.

It had been a good week for Moire. Jacques Bastille and Luc Lavache had both been arrested. So had Erica Nice. The drug factory had been closed down and more arrests were expected. No wonder Moire wanted us out of the way. He was looking forward to a promotion and maybe the Croix de Guerre or whatever medal French heroes get pinned to their right nipple. The last thing Moire needed was Tim and me hanging around to tell people the part we had played.

Moire stopped at the dock and handed us our tickets as well as a packed lunch for the crossing. "France is in your debt," he said solemnly, and before either of us could stop him he had grabbed hold of Tim and planted a kiss on both cheeks.

Tim went bright red. "I know I cracked the case," he muttered. "But let's not get too friendly . . ."

"It's just the French way," I said. Even so, I made sure I shook hands with Moire. I didn't want him getting too close.

"I wish you a good journey, my friends," Moire said.

"And this time, perhaps you will be careful what you say while you are on the ship!"

"We won't be saying anything," I promised. I'd bought Tim a Tintin comic book at the harbor bookstall. He could read that on the way home.

Moire smiled. *"Au revoir,"* he said.

"Where?" Tim asked. I'd have to translate it for him later.

We were about halfway home, this time chopping up and down on the Channel, when Tim suddenly looked up from the Tintin book. "You know," he said. "We never did find out how Erica Nice was smuggling the drugs on the train."

"Haven't you guessed?" I sighed and pulled out the blue sugar packet that had started the whole thing. It was the packet Tim had been given at the Gare du Nord. Somehow I'd never quite gotten around to opening it. I did so now.

There was a spoonful of white powder inside.

"Sugar?" Tim muttered.

"I don't think so, Tim," I replied. "This is just one packet. But Erica Nice was transporting thousands of them every day on the train. A little parcel of drugs. One dose, already weighed and perfectly concealed." I tore open the packet and held it up. The powder was caught in the wind and snatched away. I watched it go, a brief flurry of white as it skimmed over the handrail and disappeared into the gray water of the English Channel.

"Do you think we ought to tell Moire?" Tim asked.

"I expect he's worked it out for himself," I said.

In the distance I could see the white cliffs of Dover looming up. We had only been away for a week but somehow it seemed a lot longer. I was glad to be home.

Tim was still holding the packed lunch that Moire had given us. Now he opened it. The first thing he took out was a strawberry yogurt.

"Very funny," I said.

The yogurt followed the drugs into the Channel. Then we went downstairs to order fish and chips.

I KNOW WHAT YOU DID LAST WEDNESDAY

CONTENTS

AN INVITATION

I like horror stories—but not when they happen to me. If you've read my other adventures, you'll know that I've been smothered in concrete, thrown in jail with a dangerous lunatic, tied to a railway line, almost blown up, chased through a cornfield dodging machine-gun bullets, poisoned in Paris . . . and all this before my fourteenth birthday. It's not fair. I do my homework. I brush my teeth twice a day. Why does everyone want to kill me?

But the worst thing that ever happened to me began on a hot morning in July. It was the first week of summer vacation and there I was, as usual, stuck with my big brother, Tim, the world's most unsuccessful private detective. Tim had just spent a month helping with security at the American embassy in Grosvenor Square and even now I'm not sure how he'd decided that there was a bomb in the ambassador's car. Anyway, just as the ambassador was about to get in, Tim had grabbed hold of him and hurled him out of the way—which would have been heroic if there had been a bomb (there wasn't) and if Tim hadn't managed to throw the unfortunate man in front of a passing bus. The ambassador was now in the hospital. And Tim was out of work.

So there we were at the breakfast table with Tim reading

the morning mail while I counted out the cornflakes. We were down to our last box and it had to last us another week. That allowed us seventeen flakes each but as a treat I'd allowed Tim to keep the free toy. There was a handful of letters that morning and so far they'd all been bills.

"There's a letter from Mom," Tim said.

"Any money?"

"No . . ."

He quickly read the letter. It was strange to think that my mom and dad were still in Australia and that I would have been with them if I hadn't slipped off the plane and gone to stay with Tim. My dad was a door-to-door salesman, selling doors. He had a house in Sydney with three bedrooms and forty-seven doors. It had been two years since I had seen him.

"Mom says you're welcome to visit," Tim said. "She says the door is always open."

"Which one?" I asked.

He picked up the last letter. I could see at once that this wasn't a bill. It came in a square, white envelope made out of the sort of paper that only comes from the most expensive trees. The address was handwritten: a fountain pen, not a ballpoint. Tim weighed it in his hand. "I wonder what this is," he said.

"It's an envelope, Tim," I replied. "It's what letters come in."

"I mean . . . I wonder who it's from!" He smiled. "Maybe

it's a thank-you letter from the American ambassador."

"Why should he thank you? You threw him under a bus!"

"Yes, but I sent him a bunch of grapes in the hospital."

"Just open it, Tim," I said.

Tim grabbed hold of a knife, and—with a dramatic gesture—sliced open the mysterious envelope.

After we'd finished bandaging his left leg, we examined the contents. First, there was an invitation, printed in red ink on a thick white card.

Dear Herbert, it began. Tim Diamond was, of course, only the name he called himself. His real name was Herbert Simple.

It has been many years since we met, but I would like to invite you to a reunion of old boys and girls from St. Egbert's Comprehensive, which will take place from Wednesday, July 9th, to Friday, July 11th. I am sure you are busy but I am so excited to see you again that I will pay you $1,000 to make the journey to Scotland. I also enclose a ticket for the train.

   Your old friend,
   Rory McDougal

   Crocodile Island, Scotland

Tim tilted the envelope. Sure enough, a first-class train ticket slid out onto the table.

"That's fantastic!" Tim exclaimed. "A first-class ticket to Scotland." He examined the ticket. "And back again! That's even better!"

"Wait a minute," I said. "Who is Rory McDougal?" But even as I spoke, I thought the name was familiar.

"We were at school together, in the same class. Rory was brilliant. He came first in math. He was so clever, he passed all his exams without even reading the questions. After he left school, he invented the pocket calculator—which was just as well, because he made so much money he needed a pocket calculator to count it."

"McDougal Industries." Now I knew where I'd heard the name. McDougal had been in the newspapers. The man was a multi-Mcmillionaire.

"When did you last see him?" I asked.

"It must have been on graduation day, about ten years ago," Tim said. "He went to college, I joined the police."

Tim had spent only a year with the police but in that time the crime rate had doubled. He didn't often talk about it but I knew that he had once put together a sketch artist picture that had led to the arrest of the Archbishop of Canterbury. He'd been transferred to the mounted police but that had lasted only a few weeks before his horse resigned. Then he'd become a private detective—and of course, *he* had hardly made millions. If you added up all the money Tim had ever made and put it in a bank, the bank wouldn't even notice.

"Are you going?" I asked.

Tim flicked a cornflake toward his mouth. It disappeared over his shoulder. "Of course I'm going," he said. "Maybe McNoodle will offer me a job. Head of security on Alligator Island."

"Crocodile Island, Tim." I picked up the invitation. "What about me?"

"Sorry, kid. I didn't see your name on the envelope."

"Maybe it's under the stamp." Tim said nothing, so I went on, "You can't leave me here."

"Why not?"

"I'm only thirteen. It's against the law."

Tim frowned. "I won't tell if you won't tell."

"I will tell."

"Forget it, Nick. McStrudel is my old schoolfriend. He went to my old school. It's my name on the envelope and you can argue all you like. But this time, I'm going alone."

We left King's Cross station on the morning of the ninth.

Tim sat next to the window, looking sulky. I was sitting opposite him. I had finally persuaded him to swap the first-class ticket for two second-class ones, which at least allowed me to travel free. You may think it strange that I should have wanted to join Tim on a journey heading several hundred miles north. But there was something about the invitation that bothered me. Maybe it was the letter, written in ink the color of blood. Maybe it was the name—Crocodile Island.

And then there was the money. The invitation might have sounded innocent enough, but why was McDougal paying Tim $1,000 to get on the train? I had a feeling that there might be more to this than a school reunion. And for that matter, why would anyone in their right mind want to be reunited with Tim?

I was also curious. It's not every day that you get to meet a man like Rory McDougal. Computers, camcorders, mobile phones, and DVD players . . . they all came stamped with the initials RM. And every machine that sold made McDougal a little richer.

Apparently the man was something of a recluse. A few years back he'd bought himself an island off the Scottish coast, somewhere to be alone. There had been pictures of it in all the newspapers. The island was long and narrow with two arms jutting out and a twisting tail. Apparently, that was how it had gotten its name.

Tim didn't say much on the journey. To cheer him up, I'd bought him a comic book and perhaps he was having trouble with the long words. It took us about four hours to get to Scotland and it took another hour before I noticed. There were no signs, no frontier post, no man in a kilt playing the bagpipes and munching haggis as the train went past. It was only when the ticket collector asked us for our tickets and Tim couldn't understand a word he was saying that I knew we must be close. Sure enough, a few minutes later the train slowed down and Tim got out.

Personally, I would have waited until the train had actually stopped, but I suppose he was overexcited.

Fortunately he was only bruised and we managed the short walk down to the harbor, where an old fishing boat was waiting for us. The boat was called the *Silver Medal* and a small crowd of people was waiting to go on board.

"My God!" one of them exclaimed. "It's Herbert Simple! I never thought I'd see *him* again!"

The man who had spoken was fat and bald, dressed in a three-piece suit. If he ate much more, it would soon be a four-piece suit. His pants were already showing the strain. His name, it turned out, was Eric Draper. He was a lawyer.

Tim smiled. "I changed my name," he announced. "It's Tim Diamond now."

They all had a good laugh at that.

"And who is he?" Eric asked. I suddenly realized he was looking at me.

"That's my kid brother, Nick."

"So what are you doing now . . . Tim?" one of the women asked in a high-pitched voice. She had glasses and long, curly hair and such large teeth that she seemed to have trouble closing her mouth. Her name was Janet Rhodes.

Tim put on his "don't mess with me" face. Unfortunately, it just made him look seasick. "Actually," he drawled, "I'm a private detective."

"Really?" Eric roared with laughter. His suit shuddered and one of the buttons flew off. "I can't believe Rory invited you here, too. As I recall, you were the stupidest boy at St. Egbert's. I still remember your performance as Hamlet in the school play."

"What was so stupid about that?" I asked.

"Nothing. Except everyone else was doing *Macbeth*."

One of the other women stepped forward. She was small and drab-looking, dressed in a mousy coat that had seen better days. She was eating a chocolate bar. "Hello . . . Tim!" she said shyly. "I bet you don't remember me!"

"Of course I remember you!" Tim exclaimed. "You're Lisa Beach!"

"No I'm not! I'm Sylvie Binns." She looked disappointed. "You gave me my first kiss behind the bike shed. Don't you remember?"

Tim frowned. "I remember the bike shed . . ." he said.

There was a loud blast from the boat and the captain appeared, looking over the side. He had one leg, one eye, and a huge beard. All that was missing was the parrot. "All aboard!" he shouted. "Departing for Crocodile Island!"

We made our way up the gangplank. The boat was old and smelly. So was the captain. The eight of us stood on the deck while he pulled up the anchor, and a few minutes later we were off, the engine rattling as if it was about to fall out of the boat. It occurred to me that the *Silver Medal* was a strange choice of boat for a multimillionaire. What had happened to the deluxe yacht? But nobody else had noticed, so I said nothing.

Apart from Eric, Janet, and Sylvie, there were three other people on board: two more women and another man, a fit-looking black guy dressed in jeans and a sweatshirt.

"That's Mark Tyler," Tim told me as we cut through the waves, leaving the mainland behind us. "He came first in sports at St. Egbert's . . ."

I knew the name. Tyler had been on the British Olympic team in Atlanta.

"He used to run to school and run home again," Tim went on. "He was so fast, he used to overtake the school bus. When he went cross-country running, he actually left the country, which certainly made the headmaster very cross. He's a brilliant sportsman!"

That just left the two other women.

Brenda Blake was an opera singer and looked it. Big and muscular, she had the sort of arms you'd expect to find on a Japanese wrestler—or perhaps around his belly.

Libby Goldman was big and blond and worked in children's TV, hosting a television program called *Libby's Lounge*. She sang, danced, juggled, and did magic tricks . . . and all this before we'd even left the dock. It was a shame that in real life we couldn't turn her off.

The journey took about an hour, by which time the coast of Scotland had become just a gray smudge behind us. Slowly Crocodile Island sneaked up on us. It was about half a mile long, rising to a point at what must have been its "tail," with sheer cliffs sweeping down into the sea. There were six jagged pillars of rock at this end, making a landing impossible. But at the other end, in the shelter of the crocodile's arm, someone had built a jetty. As the boat drew in, I noticed a security camera watching us from above.

"Here we are, ladies and gentlemen," the captain announced from somewhere behind his beard. "I wish you all a very pleasant stay on Crocodile Island. I do indeed! I'll be coming back for you in a couple of days. My name is Captain Randle, by the way. Horatio Randle. It's been a pleasure having you lovely people on my boat. You remember me, now!"

"Aren't you coming with us?" Eric demanded.

"No, sir. I'm not invited," Captain Randle replied. "I live on the mainland. But I'll be back to collect you in a couple of days. I'll see you then!"

We disembarked. The boat pulled out and headed back the way it had come. The eight of us were left on the island, wondering what was going to happen next.

"So where's old Rory?" Brenda asked.

"Maybe we should walk up to the house," Sylvie suggested. She was the only one of them who didn't have a full-time job. She had told Tim that she was a housewife, and was carrying three photographs of her husband and three more of her house.

"Bit of a pain," Eric muttered. From the look of him, walking wasn't something he did often.

"Best foot forward!" Janet said cheerily. Apparently she

worked as a hairdresser, and her own hair was dancing in the wind. As indeed was Libby.

We walked. Sylvie might have called it a house but I would have said it was a castle that Rory had bought for himself on his island retreat. It was built out of gray brick: a grand, sprawling building with towers and battlements and even gargoyles gazing wickedly out of the corners. We reached the front door. It was solid oak, as thick as a tree and half as welcoming.

"I wonder if we should knock?" Tim asked.

"To hell with that!" Eric pushed and the door swung open.

We found ourselves in a great hall with a black-and-white floor, animal heads on the walls, and a roaring fire in the hearth. A grandfather clock chimed four times. I looked at my watch—it was actually ten past three. I was already beginning to feel uneasy. Apart from the crackle of the logs and the ticking of the clock, the house was silent. It felt empty. No Rory, no Mrs. Rory, no butler, no cook. Just us.

"Hello?" Libby called out. "Is there anyone at home?"

"It-doesn't-look-as-if-there's-anyone-here," Mark said. At least, I think that's what he said. Speaking was something else that he did very fast. Whole sentences came out of his mouth as a single word.

"This is ridiculous," Eric snapped. "I suggest we split up and try and find Rory. Maybe he's asleep upstairs."

So we all went our separate ways. Mark and Eric headed

off through different doors. Libby Goldman went into the kitchen. Tim and I went upstairs. It was only now that we were inside that I realized just how big this house was. It had five staircases, doors everywhere, and so many corridors that we could have been walking through a maze. And if it looked like a castle from the outside, inside it was like a museum. There was more furniture than you'd find in a department store. Antique chairs and sofas stood next to cupboards and sideboards and tables of every shape and size. There were so many oil paintings that you could hardly see the walls. Rory also seemed to have a fondness for ancient weapons—I had only been in the place a few minutes but already I had seen crossbows and muskets and flintlock pistols mounted on wooden plaques. On the first floor there was a stuffed bear holding an Elizabethan gun . . . a blunderbuss. The stairs and upper landing were covered in thick, red carpet that muffled every sound. In the distance I could hear Janet calling out Rory's name but it was difficult to say if she was near or far away. Suddenly we were lost and very much on our own.

We reached a corner where there was a suit of dull silver armor standing guard; a knight with a shield but no sword.

"I don't like it," I said.

"I think it's a very nice suit of armor," Tim replied.

"I'm not talking about the armor, Tim," I said. "I'm talking about the whole island. Why isn't there anyone here to meet us? And why did your friend send that old fishing boat to pick us up?"

Tim smiled. "Relax, kid," he said. "The house is a bit quiet, that's all. But my sixth sense would tell me if there was something wrong, and right now I'm feeling fine . . ."

Just then there was a high-pitched scream from another part of the second floor. It was Brenda. She screamed and screamed again.

"How lovely!" Tim exclaimed. "Brenda's singing for us! I think that's Mozart, isn't it?"

"It's not Mozart, Tim," I shouted, beginning to run toward the sound. "She's screaming for help! Come on!"

We ran down the corridor and around the corner. That was when we saw Brenda, standing in front of an open bedroom door. She had stopped screaming now but her face was white and her hands were tearing at her hair. At the same time, Libby and Sylvie appeared, coming up the stairs. And Eric was also there, pushing his way forward to see what the fuss was about.

Tim and I reached the doorway. I looked inside.

The room had a red carpet. It took me a couple of seconds to realize that the room had once had a yellow carpet. It was covered in blood. There was more blood on the walls and on the bed. There was even blood on the blood.

And there was McDougal. I'm afraid it was the end of the story for Rory. The sword that had killed him was lying next to him and I guess it must have been taken from the suit of armor.

Brenda screamed again and pulled out a handful of her own hair.

Eric stood back, gasping.

Libby burst into tears.

And Tim, of course, fainted.

There were just the eight of us, trapped on Crocodile Island. And I had to admit, our reunion hadn't gotten off to a very good start.

AFTER DARK

"It was horrible," Tim groaned. "It was horrible. Rory McPoodle . . . he was in pieces!"

"I don't want to hear about it, Tim," I said. Actually, it was too late. He'd already told me twenty times.

"Why would anyone *do* that?" he demanded. "What sort of person would do that?"

"I'm not sure," I muttered. "How about a dangerous lunatic?"

Tim nodded. "You could be right," he said.

We were sitting in our bedroom. We knew it was the bedroom that McDougal had prepared for us because it had Tim's name on the door. There were seven bedrooms on the same floor, each one of them labeled for the arriving guests. This room was square, with a high ceiling and a window with a low balcony looking out over a sea that was already gray and choppy as the sun set and the evening drew in. There was a four-poster bed, a heavy tapestry, and the sort of wallpaper that could give you bad dreams. There was also something else I'd noticed and it worried me.

"Look at this, Tim," I said. I pointed at the bedside table. "There's a telephone jack here—but no telephone. What does that tell you?"

"The last person who slept in this room stole the telephone?"

"Not exactly. I think the telephone has been taken to stop us making any calls."

"Why would anyone do that?"

"To stop us reporting the death of Rory McDougal to the police."

Tim considered. "You mean . . . someone knew we were coming . . ." he began.

"Exactly. And they also knew we'd be stuck here. At least until the boat came back."

It was a nasty thought. I was beginning to have lots of nasty thoughts, and the worst one was this: Someone had killed Rory McDougal, but had it happened before we arrived on the island? Or had he been killed by one of the people from the boat? As soon as we had arrived at the house, we had all split up. For at least ten minutes nobody had known where anybody else was, which meant that any one of us could have found Rory and killed him before the others arrived.

Along with Tim and myself, there were now six people on the island . . . six and several halves if you counted Rory. Eric Draper, Janet Rhodes, Sylvie Binns, Mark Tyler, Brenda Blake, and Libby Goldman. Tim hadn't seen any of them in ten years and knew hardly anything about them. Could one of them be a crazed killer? Could one of them have planned this whole thing?

I looked at my watch. It was ten to seven. We left the room and went back downstairs.

Eric Draper had called a meeting in the dining room at seven o'clock. I don't know who had put him in charge but I guessed he had decided himself.

"He was head boy at school," Tim told me. "He was always telling everyone what to do. Even the teachers used to do what he said."

"What was Rory McDougal like as a boy?"

"Well . . . he was young."

"That's very helpful, Tim. I mean . . . was he popular?"

"Yes. Except he once had a big fight with Libby Goldman. He tried to kiss her in biology class and she attacked him with a bicycle pump."

"But she wouldn't kill him just because of that, would she?"

"You should have seen where she put the bicycle pump!"

In fact Libby was alone in the dining room when we arrived for the meeting. She was sitting in a chair at the end of a black, polished table that ran almost the full length of the room. Portraits of bearded men in different shades of tartan looked down from the walls. A chandelier hung from the ceiling.

She looked up as we came in. Her eyes were red. Either she had been crying or she had bad hay fever—and I hadn't noticed any hay on Crocodile Island. She was smoking a cigarette—or trying to. Her hands were shaking so much she had trouble getting it into her mouth.

"What are we going to do?" she wailed. "It's so horrible! I knew I shouldn't have accepted Rory's invitation!"

"Why did you?" I asked. "If you didn't like him . . ."

"Well . . . he's interesting. He's rich. I thought he might appear on my television program—*Libby's Lounge*."

"I watch that!" Tim exclaimed.

"But it's a children's program," Libby said.

Tim blushed. "Well . . . I mean . . . I've seen it. A bit of it."

"I've never heard of it," I muttered.

Libby's eyes went redder.

Then three of the others came in: Janet Rhodes, Mark Tyler, and Brenda Blake.

"I've been trying to call the mainland on my cell phone," Janet announced. "But I can't get a signal."

"I can't get a signal either," agreed Mark, speaking as quickly as ever. He sort of shimmered in front of me and suddenly he was sitting down.

"There is no signal on this island."

"And no phone in my room," Janet said.

"No phone in any room!" The singer was looking pale and scared. Of course, she was the one who had found the body. Looking at her, I saw that it would be a few months before she sang in a concert hall. She probably wouldn't have the strength to sing in the shower.

Somewhere a clock struck seven and Eric Draper waddled into the room. "Are we all here?" he asked.

"I'm here!" Tim called out, as helpful as ever.

"I think there's one missing," I said.

Eric Draper did a quick head count. At least everyone in the room still had their heads. "Sylvie isn't here yet," he said. He scowled. You could tell he was the sort of man who expected everyone to do exactly what he said. "We'll have to wait for her."

"She was always late for everything," Janet muttered. She had slumped into a chair next to Libby. "I don't know how she managed to get the highest grades and come in first in chemistry. She was always late for class."

"I saw her in her room a few moments ago," Mark said. "She was sitting on the bed. She looked upset."

"I'm upset!" Eric said. "We're all upset! Well, let's begin without her." He cleared his throat as if we were the jury and he was about to begin his summing-up. "We are clearly in a very awkward situation here. We've been invited to this island, only to discover that our host, Rory McDougal, has been murdered. We can't call the police because it would seem that there are no telephones and none of our cell phones can get a signal. Unless we can find a boat to get back to the mainland, we're stuck here until Captain Randle—or whatever his name was—arrives to pick us up. The only good news is that there's plenty of food in the house. I've looked in the kitchen. This is a comfortable house. We should be fine here."

"Unless the killer strikes again," I said.

Everyone looked at me. "What makes you think he'll do that?" Eric demanded.

"It's a possibility," I said. "And anyway, 'he' could be a 'she.'"

I noticed Libby shivered when I said that—but to be frank she'd been shivering a lot recently.

"Did Rory invite you here, too?" Mark asked.

"Not exactly. He invited Tim, and Tim couldn't leave me on my own at home. So I came along for the ride."

Eric scowled for a second time. Scowling suited him. "I wouldn't have said this place was suitable for children," he said.

"Murder isn't suitable for children," I agreed. "But I'm stuck here with you and it seems to me that we've all been set up. No phones! That has to be on purpose. All the rooms were prepared for us, with our names on the doors. And now, like you say, we're stuck here. Suppose the killer is here, too?"

"That's not possible," Brenda whispered. But she didn't sound like she believed herself.

"Maybe Rory wasn't murdered," Tim suggested. "Maybe it was an accident."

"You mean someone accidentally chopped him to pieces?" I asked.

Janet glanced at the door. She was looking nervous. A hairdresser having a bad hair day. "Perhaps we should go and find Sylvie," she suggested.

Nobody said anything. Then, as one, we hurried out of the room.

We went back upstairs. Sylvie's room was halfway down

the corridor, two doors away from our own. It was closed. Tim knocked. There was no reply. "She could have fallen asleep," he said.

"Just open the door, Tim," I suggested.

He opened it. Sylvie's room was a similar size to ours but with more modern furniture, an abstract painting on the wall, and two single beds. Her suitcase was standing beside the wall, unopened. As my eyes traveled toward her, I noticed a twist of something silver lying in the middle of the yellow carpet. But I didn't have time to mention it.

Sylvie was lying on her back, one hand flung out. When I had first seen her I had thought her small and silent. Now she was smaller and dreadfully still. I felt Mark push past me, entering the room.

"Is she . . . ?" he began.

"Yes," Tim said. "She's asleep."

"I don't think so, Tim," I said.

Eric went over to her and took her wrist between a pudgy finger and thumb. "She has no pulse," he said. He leaned over her. "She's not breathing."

Tim's mouth fell open. "Do you think she's ill?" he asked.

"She's dead, Tim," I said. Two murders in one day. And it wasn't even Tim's bedtime.

Libby burst into tears. It was getting to be a habit with her. At least Brenda didn't scream again. At this close range, I'm not sure my eardrums could have taken it.

"What are we going to do?" someone asked. I wasn't

sure who it was and it didn't matter anyway. Because right then I didn't have any idea.

"It might have been a heart attack," Tim said. "Maybe the shock of what happened to Rory . . ."

Darkness had fallen on Crocodile Island. It had slithered across the surface of the sea and thrown itself over the house. Now and then a full moon came out from behind the clouds and for a moment the waves would ripple silver before disappearing into inky blackness. Tim and I were sitting on our four-poster bed. It looked like we were going to have to share it. Two posters each.

Maybe it had been a heart attack. Maybe she had died of fright. Maybe she'd caught a very bad case of flu. Everyone had their own ideas . . . but I knew better. I remembered the twist of silver I had seen on the carpet.

"Tim, what can you tell me about Sylvie Binns?" I asked.

"Not a lot." Tim fell silent. "She was good at chemistry."

"I know that."

"She used to go out with Mark. We always thought the two of them would get married, but in the end she met someone else. Mark ran all the way around England. That was his way of forgetting her."

Mark Tyler had been the last person to see Sylvie alive. I wondered if he really had forgotten her. Or forgiven her.

"Maybe she was ill before she came to the island," Tim muttered.

"Tim, I think she was poisoned," I said.

"Poisoned?"

I remembered my first sight of Sylvie, on the dock. She had been eating a chocolate bar. "Sylvie liked sweets and chocolate," I said.

"You're right, Nick! Yes. She loved chocolate. She could never resist it. When Mark was going out with her, he took her on a tour of a chocolate factory. She even ate the tickets." Tim frowned. "But what's that got to do with anything?"

"There was a piece of silver paper on the floor in her room. I think it was the wrapper off a piece of candy or a chocolate. Don't you see? Someone knew she couldn't resist chocolate—so they left one in her room. Maybe on her pillow."

"And it wasn't almond crunch," Tim muttered darkly.

"More likely cyanide surprise," I said.

We got into bed. Tim didn't want to turn off the lights, but a few minutes later, after he had dozed off, I reached for the switch and lay back in the darkness. I needed to think. Sylvie had eaten a poisoned chocolate. I was sure of it. But had she been given it or had she found it in her room? If it was already in the room, it could have been left there before we arrived. But if she had been given it, then the killer must still be on the island. He or she might even be in the house.

There was a movement at the window.

At first I thought I'd imagined it, but propping myself up in the bed, I saw it again. There was somebody there! No—

that was impossible. We were on the first floor. Then I remembered. There was a terrace running along the outside of the house, connecting all the bedrooms.

There it was again. I stared in horror. There was a face staring at me from the other side of the glass, a hideous skull with hollow eyes and grinning, tombstone teeth. The bones glowed in the moonlight. Now I'll be honest with you. I don't scare easily. But right then I was frozen. I couldn't move. I couldn't cry out. I'm almost surprised I didn't wet the bed.

The skull hovered in front of me. I couldn't see a body. It had to be draped in black. It's a mask, I told myself. Someone is trying to frighten you with a joke-shop mask. Somehow, I managed to force back the fear. I jerked up in bed and threw back the covers. Next to me, Tim woke up.

"Is it breakfast already?" he asked.

I ignored him. I was already darting toward the window. But at that moment, the moon vanished behind another cloud and the darkness fell. By the time I had found the lock and opened the window, the man—or woman, whoever it was—had gone.

"What is it, Nick?" Tim demanded.

I didn't answer. But it seemed that whoever had killed Rory McDougal and Sylvie Binns was still on the island.

Which left me wondering—who was going to be next?

SEARCH PARTY

Janet Rhodes didn't make it to breakfast.

There were just the five of us, sitting in the kitchen with five bowls of cornflakes and a steaming plate of scrambled eggs that Brenda had insisted on cooking but that nobody felt like eating. Libby had another cigarette in her mouth but everyone had complained so much that she wasn't smoking it. She was sucking it. Eric was still in his robe, a thick red thing with his initials—ED—embroidered on the pocket. Mark was wearing a track suit. A security camera winked at us from one corner of the room. There were a lot of security cameras on the island. But none of us felt even slightly secure.

"What are we going to do?" Brenda asked. I got the feeling that she hadn't slept very much the night before. There were dark rings under her eyes, and although she'd put on lipstick, most of it had missed her lips. "This island is haunted!" she went on.

"What do you mean?" Eric asked.

"Last night . . . my window . . . it was horrible."

"I've got quite a nice window," Tim said.

"I mean . . . I saw something! A human skull. It was dancing in the night air."

So she'd seen it, too! I was about to chip in, but then Eric interrupted. "I don't think it's going to help, sharing our bad dreams," he said.

"I didn't dream it," Brenda insisted.

"We've got to do something!" Mark cut in. "First Rory, then Sylvie. At this rate, there won't be any of us left by lunchtime."

"I don't want any lunch," Libby muttered.

"We need to talk about this," Eric said. "We need to work something out. But there's no point starting until we're all here." He glanced at the clock. "Where the hell is Janet?"

"Maybe she's in the bath," Tim suggested.

"In the water or underneath it?" Eric growled.

The minute hand on the kitchen clock ticked forward. It was nine o'clock. Suddenly Mark stood up. "I'm going upstairs," he announced.

"You're going back to bed?" Tim asked.

"I'm going to find her."

He left the room. The rest of us followed him, tiptoeing up the stairs and along the corridor with a sense of dread. Actually, Eric didn't exactly tiptoe. He was so fat that it must have been quite a few years since his toes had tips. Mark Tyler had moved quickly, taking the stairs four at a time as if they were hurdles and he was back at the Olympic Games in Atlanta. He was outside the door when we arrived.

"She's overslept," Tim said to me. "She's fine. She's just overslept."

Eric knocked on her door. There was no answer. He knocked again, then turned the handle. The door opened.

The hairdresser had overslept all right, but nothing was ever going to wake her up again. She had been stabbed during the night. She was lying on her back on a four-poster bed like the one in our room, only smaller. The bed was old. The paint had peeled off the posts and there was a tear in the canopy above her. In fact the whole room looked shabby, as if it had been left out by the decorators. Maybe I noticed all this because I didn't want to look at the body. You may think I'm crazy, but dead people upset me. And when I did finally look at her, I got a shock.

Whoever had killed her hadn't used a knife. There was something sticking out of her chest and at first I thought it was some sort of rocket. It was silver, in the shape of a sort of long pyramid, with four legs jutting out. Then, slowly, it dawned on me what I was looking at. It was a model, a souvenir of the building that I had climbed up with Tim only the year before.

It was incredible. But true. Janet Rhodes had been stabbed with a model of the Eiffel Tower.

"The Eiffel Tower!" Tim muttered. His face was the color of sour milk. "It's an outrage. I mean, it's meant to be a tourist attraction!"

"Why the Eiffel Tower?" I asked.

"Because it's famous, Nick. People like to visit it."

"No—I don't mean, why is it a tourist attraction. I mean, why use it as a murder weapon? It's certainly a strange choice. Maybe someone is trying to tell us something."

"Well, they certainly told Janet something," Tim said.

We were back at the breakfast table. The scrambled eggs were cold and congealed and looked even less appetizing than before. All the cornflakes had gone soggy. But it didn't matter. There was no way anybody was going to eat anything today. The way things were going, I wondered if any of us would ever eat anything again.

Nobody was talking very much. I knew why. But it was Brenda who put it into words.

"Do you realize . . ." she began, and for once her voice was hoarse and empty. "Do you realize that the killer could be sitting here, at this table?"

Tim looked around. "But there's only us here!"

"That's what she means, Tim," I said. "She's saying that the killer could be one of us!"

Brenda nodded. "I know it's one of us. One of us got up last night and went down the corridor." She shuddered. "I thought I heard squeaking last night . . ."

"That was Tim," I said. "He snores."

"No. It was a floorboard. Somebody left their room . . ."

"Did anyone else hear anything last night?" Eric asked.

There was a pause. Then Libby nodded. "I have the room next to Mark," she said. She turned to look at him. "I heard your door open just after midnight. I heard you go into the corridor."

"I went to the toilet," Mark replied. His dark face had suddenly got darker. He didn't like being accused.

"You went to the toilet in the corridor?" Tim asked.

"I went to the toilet which is across the corridor, opposite my room. I didn't go anywhere near Janet."

"What about the skull?" Brenda whispered. Eric scowled. He had forgotten about the dancing skull. "I know you say it's a dream, Eric," she went on. "But that's typical of you. You never believed anything I said, even when we were at school. Well, believe me now . . ." She took a deep breath. "Maybe it wasn't a ghost or a monster. Maybe it was someone in a mask. But they were there! I was awake. I jumped out of bed and went over to the window but by the time I got there, seconds later, they'd gone. Vanished into thin air . . ."

"It wasn't a dream," I said. "I saw it, too."

"You?" Eric sneered at me.

I nodded.

"I didn't see anything," Tim said.

"You were asleep, Tim. But it was definitely there. It came out of nowhere . . . like a magic trick. A rabbit out of a hat!"

"You saw a rabbit, too?" Tim asked.

We all ignored him. "Any one of us could have climbed out onto the terrace," Brenda said. "Any one of us could have killed Janet. And Rory. And Sylvie! How do we know that she wasn't strangled or poisoned or something?"

"I think she *was* poisoned," I said.

Everyone looked at me, so I told them about the candy wrapper and Sylvie's love of chocolate. It was strange. Everyone in the room was years older than me but suddenly I was in control.

Not for long, though. Eric Draper, the ex–head boy, raised his hands. "Ladies and gentlemen," he announced. "I don't think we should jump to conclusions. Why would any of us sitting at this table want to kill Rory or Sylvie or Janet?"

"Mark used to go out with Sylvie," Libby said. She was staring at him. "When she broke up with you, you told me you wanted to kill her."

"That was ten years ago!" Mark protested. He jerked a finger at Libby. "Anyway, what about *you*? You nearly *did* kill Rory with that bicycle pump . . ."

"Yes. And what about you!" Tim pointed at Eric. "You say your name's Eric, so why are you wearing a robe that belongs to Ed?"

It took Eric a few seconds to work out what Tim was getting at. "Those are my initials, you idiot!" he snapped. He took a deep breath and raised his hands. "Look," he went on. "There's no point arguing among ourselves. We have to stick together. It could be our only hope."

The others fell silent. I had to admit, Eric was speaking sense. Blaming one another wouldn't help.

"Both Brenda and . . . Tim's little brother saw somebody last night," he went on. I didn't know why he couldn't call me by my name. "Now that could have been one of us, dressing up to frighten the others. But remember, we were all inside the house . . . and this thing, whatever it was, was outside. So maybe it was someone else. Maybe it was someone we don't know about."

"You mean . . . someone hiding on the island?" Mark said.

"Exactly. We know we can't call the police. We know we're stuck here. But it seems to me that the first thing we have to do is find out if there's anyone else here."

"We've got to organize a search party," I said.

Tim shook his head. "This is no time for a party, Nick," he muttered.

"You're right, Eric," Libby said. "We've got to go over the island from head to tail."

"But at the same time, I think we should keep an eye on each other," Brenda said. "I'll feel safer that way."

Eric went upstairs to get changed. Mark went with him. From now on, we were going to do everything in pairs. Brenda and Libby cleared the breakfast things. I'd already noticed that most of the food in the house was canned— which was just as well. Even the cleverest killer couldn't tamper with a can, so at least we wouldn't starve. At half past nine we all met in the hall. Then we put on our coats and went outside.

The search began back at the jetty, right at the head of the crocodile. The idea was that we could cover the entire island, working like the police searching woods when someone has disappeared. That is, we kept thirty feet apart, always in sight of one another, moving across the island in a line. It was a beautiful day. The sun was shining and the sea was blue, but even so I could feel a chilly breeze on Crocodile Island. And there was something else. I couldn't escape the feeling that I was being watched. It was weird. Because it was obvious that there wasn't anybody in sight . . . not even so much as a sheep or a cow.

It took us only an hour to cover the island. There really wasn't very much there. Most of it was covered in grass and shrubs that only came up to the knee, which no killer could have hidden behind—unless, of course, he happened to be extremely small. There were a few trees but we checked the branches and Tim even climbed one to see if anyone was hiding at the top. Then I climbed up to help Tim down again and we moved on. We came to a couple of ruined outbuildings. I went inside. There was nobody there—but I did see something. Another security camera, fixed to the brickwork. Of course, a rich man like Rory would have had to be careful about security. I remembered the camera I had noticed in the kitchen. He had probably covered the whole island. Was that why I had felt we were being watched?

We went past the house and continued toward the crocodile's tail. The ground rose steeply up, finally arriving at a narrow point at least sixty feet above the sea. This was what I had seen from the boat. Six great rocks, steel gray and needle-sharp, rose out of the water far below. Looking down made my head spin. I wondered briefly if there might be a cave somewhere, perhaps tucked underneath the lip where we were standing. But then a wave rolled in, crashing against the cliff face. If there was a killer down there, he'd be soaking wet. And anyway, as far as I could see, there was no way down.

We moved away, retracing our steps. There was nobody outside the house, but how about inside? Starting in the hall, we went from room to room: the library, the dining room, the conservatory, the hall, and so on. We looked behind curtains, under tables, in the fireplaces, and up the chimneys. Tim even looked in the grandfather clocks. Maybe he thought he'd find somebody's grandfather. We covered the ground floor and then went up to the first. Here were the bedrooms, with our names still attached to the doors. We went into every one of them. There was nobody there . . . apart from the three very dead bodies. It wasn't easy searching those particular rooms, but we made ourselves . . . although I think Tim was wasting his time doing it with his eyes tightly shut.

Nobody in the rooms. Nobody in the corridors. We found the attic but all that was there was a water tank. Tim dipped his head in and I made a mental note not to drink any more water. Not with his dandruff. Eventually, we gave up. We had been everywhere. There was nowhere else to look.

We started to go back down to the kitchen but had only gotten halfway there when Libby let out a little gasp.

"What is it?" Eric demanded.

"There." She pointed at the wall at the end of the corridor. "I don't know why I didn't see it before!"

What she had seen was a black-and-white photograph in a silver frame. It was hanging right in the middle of the wall with enough space around it to make it stand out. The question was—had Rory hung it there? Or had it been someone else? Was this something we were meant to see?

The photograph showed nine teenagers, all of them wearing the same uniform. It's funny how people change in ten years—but I recognized them at once: Eric Draper, Janet Rhodes, Mark Tyler, Brenda Blake, Sylvie Binns, Libby Goldman, Rory McDougal, and Tim. Tim looked the weirdest of them all. He'd had long hair then, and acne. Lots of acne. Of course, I wouldn't have looked too great myself when the picture had been taken—but then I would only have been a baby.

There was one face, however, that I didn't know. He was standing at the edge of the group, slightly apart—a thin, gangly teenager with curly hair and glasses. He was wearing a windbreaker and had the sort of face you'd expect to see on a train-spotter. "Who's he?" I asked.

"That's Johnny!" Brenda replied. "Johnny Nadler. He was one of my best friends . . ."

"And mine," Libby agreed. "Everyone liked Johnny. We used to hang out with him in the yard." She walked closer to the photograph. "I remember when this was taken. It was graduation day, when they handed out awards. He came in second in geography. I came in first."

"Wait a minute," I interrupted. "Everyone in this photograph is here on Crocodile Island. Everyone except Johnny Nadler!"

"You're right!" Mark agreed. "Why wasn't he invited?"

"Because he's the killer!" Eric snapped. "He's got to be!"

"But why would Johnny want to kill Rory?" Brenda asked. "The two of them were friends. And every day after school he used to catch the bus with Sylvie—even though it took him eight miles in the wrong direction. That's how much he liked her."

"He let Janet cut his hair," Libby went on. "She accidentally cut a chunk out of his ear, but he didn't mind. In fact he laughed all the way to the hospital. Johnny wouldn't hurt anyone."

"What else can you tell me about him?" I asked.

"He came in second in history as well as geography," Eric said. "He was really clever."

"He was always playing with model planes and cars," Mark added. "He used to build them himself. We always said he'd be an inventor when he left school but in fact he ended up working at a pharmacy. I saw him there once, when I went in to get some ointment." He blushed. "I had athlete's foot."

"Did any of the rest of you ever see him again?" I asked. Everyone shook their heads. I looked at the photograph again. It did seem strange that he was the only one in the picture who hadn't been invited to Crocodile Island. But did that make him the killer? And if so, where on earth was he? We had searched the entire island and we were certain now that we were the only ones who were there.

Eric looked at his watch. It was half past twelve. "I suggest we continue this meeting downstairs," he said.

"I need to change," Brenda said.

"Me too," Libby agreed.

Everyone started to move in different directions.

"Hold on a minute!" I said. "I thought we were all going to stick together. I think we should all stay in this room."

"Don't be ridiculous!" Eric snapped. "We have to eat something. It's lunchtime. And anyway, we've just searched the island. We know there's nobody else here."

"Well, I'm staying with Tim," I said.

"How do you know I'm not the killer?" Tim demanded.

Because whoever killed Rory and the others is brilliant and fiendish and you still have trouble tying your shoelaces. That was what I thought, but I didn't say anything. I just shrugged.

"I don't want to be near anyone," Libby said. "I feel safer on my own."

"Me, too." Brenda nodded. "And I'm certainly not having anyone in the room with me while I'm changing."

"We can meet in ten minutes," Eric said. "We're inside the house. We know there's nobody else on the island. We'll meet in the dining room at twenty to one."

He was wrong of course. This was one little group that was never going to meet again. But how could we know that? We were scared and we weren't thinking straight.

Tim and I went back to our room. Tim scratched his head, which was still damp from the water tank. "Johnny could be hiding on the island," he said. "What if there's a secret room?"

The same thought had already occurred to me, but I'd tapped every wall and every wooden panel and nothing had sounded hollow. "I don't think there are any secret rooms, Tim," I said.

"But you can't be sure . . ." Tim began to tap his way along the wall, his eyes half-closed, listening for a hollow sound. A few moments later, he straightened up, excited. "There's definitely something on the other side here!" he cried.

"I know, Tim," I said. "That's the window."

I left him in the bedroom, drying his hair, and went back downstairs. I was going to join the others in the dining room. But I never got that far. I was about halfway down when I heard it. A short, sudden scream. Then a crashing sound. It had come from somewhere outside.

I ran down the rest of the way, through the hall and out the front door. Mark Tyler appeared, running around the side of the house.

"What was it . . . ?" he demanded. He was trying not to sound scared but it wasn't working.

"Around the back?"

We went there together, moving more slowly now, knowing what we were going to find, not wanting to find it. The kitchen door opened and Brenda Blake came out. I noticed she was breathing heavily.

This time it was Libby Goldman. I'm afraid she had taped her last episode of *Libby's Lounge* and for her the final credits were already rolling. Why had she gone outside? Maybe she'd decided to light up one of her cigarettes—in which case, this was one time when smoking certainly had been bad for her health. Fatal, in fact. But it hadn't been the tobacco that had killed her. Something had hit her hard on the head: something that had been dropped from above. I looked up, working out the angles. We were directly underneath the battlements. Behind them, the roof was flat. It would have been easy enough for someone to hide up there, to wait for any one of us to step outside. Libby must have come out to get a breath of fresh air before the meeting. Air wasn't something she'd be needing again.

There were footsteps on the gravel. Eric and Tim had arrived. They stared in silence. Mark stretched out a finger and pointed. It took me a minute to work out what he was pointing at. That was how much his finger was trembling.

And there it was, lying in the grass. At first I didn't recognize the object that had been dropped from the roof and that had fallen right onto Libby Goldman. I mean, I knew what it was—but I couldn't believe that that was what had been used.

It was a big round ball: a globe. The sort of thing you find in a library. Maybe it had been in Rory's library before the killer had carried it up to the roof. The United States of America was facing up. It was stained red.

I looked at Eric Draper. His mouth had dropped open. He looked genuinely shocked. Mark Tyler was standing opposite him, staring. Brenda Blake was to one side. She was crying.

One of them had to be faking it. I was certain of it. One of them had to have climbed down from the room after watching Libby fall. There was nobody else here. One of them had to be the killer.

But which one?

MORE MURDER

Eric Draper? Brenda Blake? Or Mark Tyler?

It was early evening and Tim and I had gone for a walk—supposedly to clear our heads. But the truth was, I wanted to be alone with him and somehow I felt safer away from the house. It struck me that all the deaths had taken place inside or near the building. And if we stayed too close to the house something else might strike me—a falling piano or a model of the Taj Mahal, for example.

I glanced down at the piece of paper I was holding in my hand. I had made a few notes just before we left:

RORY McDOUGAL—Killed with a sword.
SYLVIE BINNS—Poisoned.
JANET RHODES—Stabbed with an Eiffel Tower!
LIBBY GOLDMAN—Knocked down with a globe.

There was a pattern in there somewhere but I just couldn't see it. Maybe some fresh air would help after all.

"I've got an idea!" Tim said.

"Go ahead, Tim," I said.

"Maybe I could swim back over to the coast and get some help."

We were sitting on the jetty. Today the sea was flat, the waves caught as if in a photograph. I could just make out the mainland, a vague ribbon lying on the horizon. The sun was setting fast. How many of us would see it rise again?

I shook my head. "No, Tim. It's too far."

"It can't be more than five miles."

"And you can't swim."

"Oh yes. I'd forgotten." He glanced at me. "But you can."

"I can't swim five miles!" I said. "The water's too cold. And there's too much of it. No. Our only hope is to solve this before the killer strikes again."

"You're right, Nick." Tim closed his eyes and sat in silence for a minute. Then he opened them again. "Maybe we could get one of the others to swim . . ."

"One of the others *is* the killer!" I said. "I saw someone out on the terrace, wearing a skeleton mask. I don't know how they managed to disappear so quickly—but I wasn't imagining it. Brenda saw them, too."

"Maybe it was Mark! He's a fast mover."

"And just now . . . when Libby Goldman was killed. Someone must have climbed up onto the roof." I thought back. "Brenda was out of breath when she came into the garden . . ."

"She could have been singing!"

"I doubt it. But she could have been running. She drops the globe, then runs all the way downstairs . . ."

A seagull flew overhead, crying mournfully. I knew how it felt. I almost wanted to cry myself.

"What's missing is the motive," I went on. "Think back, Tim. You were at school with these people. There are only three of them left—Brenda, Mark, and Eric. Would any of them have any reason to kill the rest of you?"

Tim sighed. "The only people who ever threatened to kill me," he said, "were the teachers. My French teacher once threw a piece of chalk at me. And when that missed, he threw the blackboard."

"How did you get on with Mark Tyler?"

"We were friends. We used to sit next to each other in chemistry lessons." He scratched his head. "I did have a little accident once, but he was able to laugh about it. Once we'd put out the flames. And I visited him lots of times in the hospital."

"How about Brenda Blake?"

Tim thought back. "She was in the school choir," he said. "She was also on the soccer team. She used to sing on the bench." He scratched his head. "We used to tease her a bit but it was never serious."

"Maybe she didn't agree."

The waves rolled in toward us. I looked out at the mainland, hoping to catch sight of Horatio Randle and his boat, the *Silver Medal*. But the sea was empty, darkening as the sun dipped behind it. What had the old fisherman said when he'd dropped us? *"I'll be back in a couple of days."* It had been Wednesday when we arrived. He might not return until the weekend. How many passengers would there be left waiting for him?

"How about Eric Draper?" I asked.

"What about him?"

"He could be the killer. It would have to be someone strong to carry the globe up to the roof in the first place. Can you remember anything about him?"

Tim laughed. "He was a great sport. I'll never forget the last day of the term when the seven of us pulled off his pants and threw him in the canal!"

"What?" I exclaimed. "You pulled off his pants and threw him in the canal? Why?"

"Well, he was the head boy. And he'd always been bossy. It was just a bit of fun. Except that he nearly drowned. And the canal was so polluted, he had to spend six months in the hospital."

"Are you telling me that the seven of you nearly killed Eric?" I was almost screaming. "Hasn't it occurred to you that this whole thing could be his revenge?"

"But it was just a joke!"

"You almost killed him, Tim! Maybe he wasn't amused."

I stood up. It was time to go back to the house. The other three would be waiting for us . . . if they'd managed to survive the last half hour.

"I wish I'd never come here," Tim muttered.

"I wish you'd never come here," I agreed.

"Poor Libby. And Sylvie. And Janet. And Rory, of course. He was first."

We walked a few more steps in silence. Then I suddenly stopped. "What did you say, Tim?" I demanded.

"I didn't say anything!"

"Yes, you did! Before you weren't saying anything, you were saying something."

"I asked which side of the bed you wanted."

"No. That was yesterday." I played back what he had just said and that was when I saw it, the pattern I'd been looking for. "You're brilliant!" I said.

"Thanks!" Tim frowned. "What have I done?"

"Tell me," I said. "Did Libby come in first in anything at school? And was it . . . by any chance . . . geography?"

"Yes. She did. How did you know?"

"Let's get back inside," I said.

I found Eric, Mark, and Brenda in the drawing room. This was one of the most extraordinary rooms in the house—almost like a chapel with a great stained-glass window at one end and a high, vaulted ceiling. Rory McDougal had obviously fancied himself as a musician. There was even a church organ against the wall, the silver pipes looming over us. Like so many of the other rooms, the walls were lined with old weapons. In here they were antique pistols; muskets and flintlocks. All in all, we couldn't have chosen a worse house to share with a mass murderer. There were more weapons than you'd find in the Tower of London and I just hoped that they weren't as real as they looked.

The three survivors were sitting in heavy, leather chairs. I stood in front of them with the organ on one side and a row of bookshelves on the other. Everyone was watching me and I felt a bit like Sherlock Holmes at the end of one of his cases, explaining it to the suspects. The only trouble was, this wasn't the end of the case. I was still certain that I was talking to the murderer. He or she had to be one of the people in the room.

Somewhere outside, a clock chimed the hour. It was nine o'clock. Night had fallen.

"Seven of you were invited to Crocodile Island," I began. "And I see now that you all have something in common."

"We went to the same school," interrupted Tim.

"I know that, Tim. But there's something else. You all got prizes for coming in first in certain subjects. You've already told me that Rory was first in math. Libby was first in geography . . ."

"What's this got to do with anything?" Eric snapped.

"Don't you see? Libby was first in geography and someone dropped a globe on her head. Someone told me that Sylvie Binns came in first in chemistry and we think she was poisoned."

"Janet came in first in French . . ." Mark murmured.

". . . which would explain why she was stabbed with a model of the Eiffel Tower. And Rory McDougal came in first in math."

"He was stabbed, too," Eric said.

"He was more than stabbed. He was divided!"

There was a long silence.

"That's the reason why Johnny Nadler wasn't invited to the island," Brenda said. "He never came first in anything. He was second . . ."

"But that means . . ." Eric had gone pale. "I came in first in history."

"I came in first in sports," Mark said.

Brenda nodded. "And I came in first in music."

We all turned to look at Tim. But he couldn't have come in first in anything . . . could he? I noticed he was blushing. He licked his lips and looked the other way.

"What did you come in first in, Tim?" I asked.

"I didn't . . ." he began, but I could tell he was lying.

"We have to know," I said. "It could be important."

"I remember . . ." Brenda began.

"All right," Tim sighed. "I got first prize in needlework."

"Needlework!" I exclaimed.

"Well . . . yes. It was a hobby of mine. Just for a bit. I mean . . ." He was going redder and redder. "I didn't even want the prize. I just got it. It was for a handkerchief . . ."

The idea of my sixteen-year-old brother winning a prize for an embroidered hankie made my head spin. But this wasn't the time to laugh. Hopefully I'd be able to do that later.

"Wait a minute! Wait a minute!" Eric said. He looked annoyed. Maybe it was because I was younger than him and I was the one who'd worked it out. "I came in first in history— and you're saying I'm going to be killed . . . *historically*?"

"That's what it looks like," I said.

"But how . . . ?"

I pointed at the wall, at the flintlock pistols on the wooden plaques. "Maybe someone will use one of those," I said. "Or there are swords, arrows, spears . . . that bear upstairs is even holding a blunderbuss. This place is full of old weapons."

"What about me?" Brenda whispered.

"You're not an old weapon!" Tim said.

"I came first in music." Brenda glared at the organ as if it was about to jump off the wall and eat her.

"But who's *doing* this?" Mark cut in. "I mean . . . it's got to be someone in this room. Right? We know there's nobody else on the island. There can't be anybody hiding. We've searched everywhere."

"It's him!" Brenda pointed at Eric. "He never forgave us for throwing him in the canal. This is his revenge!"

"What about *you*?" Eric returned. "You once said you were going to kill us all. It was in the school yard. I remember it clearly!"

"That's true!" Mark said.

"You used to bully me all the time," Brenda wailed. "Just because I had pigtails. And crooked teeth."

"And you were fat," Tim reminded her.

"But I didn't mean it, when I said that." She turned to Mark. "You said you were going to kill Tim when he set fire to you in chemistry class."

"I only broke three of his fingers!" Tim interrupted.

"I didn't much like Tim," Mark agreed. "And you're

right. I would have quite happily strangled him. Not that it would have been easy with three broken fingers. But I never had any argument with you or with Eric or any of the others. Why would I want to kill you?"

"It's still got to be one of us," Eric insisted. He paused. "It can't be Tim," he went on.

"Why not?" Tim asked.

"Because this whole business is the work of a fiendish madman and you're not fiendish. You're just silly!"

"Oh thanks!" Tim looked away.

"I know it's not me . . ." Eric went on.

"That's what you say," Brenda sniffed.

"I know it's not me, so it's got to be Brenda or Mark."

"What about Sylvie?" Tim suggested.

"She's already dead, Tim," I reminded him quietly.

"Oh yes."

"This is all irrelevant," Mark said. "The question is—what are we going to do? We could be stuck on this island for days, or even weeks. It all depends on when Captain Randle comes back. And by then it could be too late!"

"I'd like to make a suggestion," I said. Everyone stopped and looked at me. "The first thing is, we've all got to keep each other in sight."

"The kid's right," Mark agreed. "So long as we can see each other, we're going to be safe."

"That's true!" Tim exclaimed. "All we have to do is keep our eyes open and everything will be fine." He turned to me.

"You're brilliant, Nick. For a moment there I was getting really worried."

Then all the lights went out.

It happened so suddenly that for a moment I thought it was just me. Had I been knocked out or somehow closed my eyes without noticing? The last thing I saw was the four of them—Eric, Brenda, Mark, and Tim—sitting in their chairs as if caught in a photograph. Then everything was black. There was no moon that night, and even if there had been, the stained-glass window would have kept most of the light out. Darkness came crashing onto us. It was total.

"Don't panic!" Eric said.

There was a gunshot. I saw it, a spark of red on the other side of the room.

Tim screamed and for a horrible moment I wondered if he had been shot. I forced myself to calm down. He'd come in first in needlework. Nobody would be aiming a gun at him.

"Tim!" I called out.

"Can I panic now?" he called back.

"Eric . . . ?" That was Mark's voice.

And then there was a sort of groaning sound, followed by a heavy thud. At the same time I heard a door open and close. I stood up, trying to see through the darkness. But it was hopeless. I couldn't even make out my own hand in front of my face.

"Tim?" I called again.

"Nick?" I was relieved to hear his voice.

"Eric?" I tried.

Silence.

"Brenda?"

Nothing.

"Mark?"

The lights came back on.

There were only two people alive in the room. I was standing in front of my chair. One more step and I'd have put my foot through the coffee table. Tim was *under* the coffee table. He must have crawled there when the lights went out. Eric was on the floor. He had been shot. There was a flint-lock pistol, still smoking, lying on the carpet on the other side of the room. It must have been taken off the wall, fired, and then dropped. At least, that's what it looked like. Brenda was sitting in her chair. She was dead too. One of the organ pipes—the largest—had been pulled down on top of her. That must have been the thud I had heard. Brenda had sung her last opera. The only music she needed now was a hymn.

There was no sign of Mark.

"Are you all right, Tim?" I demanded.

"Yes!" Tim sounded surprised. "I haven't been murdered!" he exclaimed.

"I noticed." I waited while he climbed out from underneath the coffee table. "At least we know who the killer is," I said.

"Do we?"

"It's got to be Mark." I said. "Mark Tyler . . ."

"I always knew it was him," Tim said. "Call it intuition. Call it experience. But I knew he was a killer even before he'd done any killing."

"I don't know, Tim," I said. It bothered me, because to be honest Mark was the last person I would have suspected. And yet, at the same time, I had to admit . . . it would have taken a fast mover to push the globe off the roof and make it all the way downstairs in time and Mark was the fastest person on the island.

"Where do you think he went?" Tim asked.

"I don't know."

We left the room carefully. In fact, Tim made me leave it first. The fact was that—unless I'd got the whole thing wrong—it was just the three of us now on the island; Mark could be waiting for us anywhere. Or waiting for Tim, rather. He had no quarrel with me. And that made me think. Tim had come in first in needlework. Following the pattern of the other deaths, that meant he would probably be killed with some sort of needle. But what would that mean? A sewing needle dipped in poison? A hypodermic?

Tim must have had the same thought. He was looking everywhere, afraid to touch anything, afraid even to take another step. We went out into the hall. The fire had died down and was glowing red. The front door was open.

"Maybe he went outside," Tim said.

"What would be the point?" I asked.

Tim shuddered. "Don't talk about points," he said.

We went outside. And that was where we found Mark. He had come in first in sports but now he had reached the finish line. Somebody had been throwing the javelin and they'd thrown it at him. It had hit him in the chest. He was lying on the grass, doing a good impersonation of a sausage on a stick.

"It's . . . it's . . . it's . . ." Tim couldn't finish the sentence.

"Yeah," I said. "It's Mark." There were a few leaves scattered around his body. That puzzled me. The nearest trees were thirty feet away. But this wasn't the time to play the detective. There were no more suspects. And only one more victim.

I looked at Tim.

Tim looked at me.

We were the only two left.

NEEDLES

Tim didn't sleep well that night. Although I hadn't said anything, not wanting to upset him, even he had managed to
work out that he had to be the next on the killer's list. He
also knew that his own murder would have something to do
with needlework. So he was looking for needles everywhere.

By one o'clock in the morning we knew that there were
no sewing needles in the room, no knitting needles, and no
pine needles. Even so, it took him an hour to get into bed
and several more hours to get to sleep. Mind you, nobody
would have found it easy getting to sleep dressed in a full
suit of medieval armor, but that still hadn't stopped Tim
from putting it on.

"There could be a poisoned needle in the mattress," he
said. "Or someone could try and inject me with a syringe."

Tim didn't snore that night; he clanked. Every time he
rolled over he sounded like twenty cans of beans in a
washing machine. I just hoped he wasn't planning to take a
bath in the suit of armor the following morning. That way he
could end up rusting to death.

At four-thirty, he woke up screaming.

"What is it, Tim?" I asked.

"I had a bad dream, Nick," he said.

"Don't tell me. You saw a needle."

"No. I saw a haystack."

I didn't sleep well either. I got a cramp and woke up in the morning with pins and needles. I didn't tell Tim, though. He'd have had a fit.

We had breakfast together in the kitchen. Neither of us ate very much. For starters, we were surrounded by dead bodies, which didn't make us feel exactly cheerful. But Tim was also terrified. I'd managed to persuade him to change out of the armor but now he was worrying about the food. Were there going to be needles in the cereal? A needle in the tea? In the end, I gave him a straw with a tissue taped over the end. The tissue worked as a filter and he was able to suck up a little orange juice and a very softly boiled egg.

I have to say that for once I was baffled. It was still like being in an Agatha Christie novel—only this time I couldn't flick through to the last page and see who did it without bothering to read the rest. Personally, I had always thought Eric had been the killer. He seemed to have the strongest motive—being half-drowned on the last day of school. It was funny really. All eight of the old boys and girls of St. Egbert's had disliked one another. But someone, some-where, had disliked them all even more. The whole thing had been planned right down to the last detail. And the last detail, unfortunately, was Tim.

But who? And why?

Tim sat miserably at his end of the table, hardly daring to

move. Why had he had to come in first in *needlework* of all things? How was I supposed to find the needle that was going to kill him? I knew now that the only hope for me was to solve this thing before the killer struck one last time. And a nasty thought had already occurred to me. Would the killer stop with Tim? I wasn't meant to be part of this. I had never gone to St. Egbert's. But I was a witness to what had happened and maybe I had seen too much.

I went over what had happened the night before. We had always assumed that there was nobody else on the island, but thinking it through, I knew this couldn't be true. We had all been sitting down: Brenda in front of the organ, Eric opposite her, Mark nearest the door, and Tim and me on the sofa. But none of us had been anywhere near the light switch, and someone had most certainly turned off the lights—not just in the drawing room but throughout the entire house. Somewhere down in the basement, there would be a main fuse switch. But that led to another question. If the killer had been down in the basement, then how had he or she managed to appear in the room seconds later to shoot Eric and push the organ pipe onto Brenda?

At the time, I had assumed that Mark had committed the last two murders. There had been a shot, then a thud, then the opening and closing of a door. But a few seconds later, Mark had himself been killed. And what about the leaves that I had seen lying next to his body? How had they gotten there?

I thought back to the other murders. Rory first. We had

all been on the island and we had all separated. Any one of us could have attacked him and, immediately afterward, left the chocolate on the bed for Sylvie to find. That was the night I had seen the face at the window. A face that had appeared and disappeared—impossibly—in seconds. And then we had found Janet. I remembered her lying in her bed, stabbed by a model of the Eiffel Tower. Her room had been shabby. There had been a tear in the canopy . . . I had noticed it at the time. Why had it caught my eye?

Libby Goldman next. The television show host had been knocked down with a model globe. There was something strange about that, too. Someone must have carried it up to the roof and dropped it on her when she came out of the front door. But now that I thought about it, I hadn't seen the globe in any of the rooms when we had been searching the house. And that could mean only one thing. It had been on the roof from the very start, waiting for her . . .

Maybe you know how it is when you've been given a particularly nasty piece of homework—an impossible equation or a fiendish bit of physics or something. You stare at it and stare at it, but it's all just ink on paper and you're about to give up when you notice something and suddenly you realize it's not so difficult after all. Well, that was what was happening to me now.

I remembered the search party, slowly crisscrossing the island. We had seen security cameras everywhere, and from the day I had arrived, I had felt that I was being watched.

There was a security camera in the kitchen. I looked up. It was watching me even now. Were there cameras in other rooms, too?

At the same time, I remembered something Mark had said, when we had found the old photograph of St. Egbert's. And in that second, as quickly as that, I suddenly knew everything.

"I've got it, Tim!" I said.

"So have I, Nick!" Tim cried.

I'd been so wrapped up in my own thoughts that I hadn't noticed Tim had been thinking, too. Now he was staring at me with the sort of look you see on a fish when it's spent too much time out of water.

"You know who did it?" I asked.

"Yes."

"Go on!"

"It's simple!" Tim explained. "First there were eight of us on the island, then seven, then six, then five . . ."

"I know," I interrupted. "I can count backward."

"Well, now there are only two of us left. I know it wasn't me who committed the murders." He reached forward and snatched up a spoon. Then he realized what he'd done, put it down, and snatched up a knife. He waved it at me. "So the killer must be you!" he exclaimed.

"What?" I couldn't believe what I was hearing.

"There's only us left. You and me. I know it wasn't me, so it must have been you."

"But why would I want to kill everyone?" I demanded. "You tell me!"

"I wouldn't! And I didn't! Don't be ridiculous, Tim."

I stood up. That was a mistake.

"Don't come near me!" Tim yelled, and suddenly he sprang out of his chair and jumped out of the window. This was an impressive feat. The window wasn't even open.

I couldn't believe what had happened. I knew Tim was stupid but this was remarkable even by his standards. Maybe sleeping in a suit of armor had done something to that tiny organism he called his brain. At the same time, I was suddenly worried. I knew who the killer was now and I knew who was lined up to be the next victim. Tim was outside the house, on his own. He had made himself into a perfect target.

I had no choice. I went after him, jumping through the shattered window. I could see Tim a short distance away, running toward the tail of Crocodile Island. I had no idea where he was going. But of course, neither did he. He was panicking—just trying to put as much distance between the two of us as he could. Not easy considering he was trapped on a small island.

"Tim!" I called.

He didn't stop. I ran after him, following the path as it began to climb steeply up toward the cliffs. This was where the island tapered to a point. I slowed down. Tim had already reached the far end. He had nowhere else to go.

The wind blew his hair around his head as he turned to face me. He was still holding the knife. I noticed now that it was a butter knife. If he stabbed me with all his strength he might just manage to give me a small bruise. His face was pale and his eyes were wide open and staring. The last time I had seen him like this was when they had shown *Jurassic Park* on TV.

"Get back, Nick!" he yelled. It was hard to hear him above the crash of the waves.

"You're crazy, Tim!" I called back. "Why would I want to hurt you? I'm your brother. Think about all the adventures we've had together! I've saved your life lots of times." I thought of telling him that I loved him but he'd have known that wasn't true. "I quite like you!" I said. "You've looked after me ever since Mom and Dad emigrated to Australia. We've had fun together!"

Tim hesitated. I could see the doubt in his eyes. He lowered the butter knife. A huge wave rolled in and crashed against the rocks, spraying us both with freezing salt water. I looked past Tim at the rocks, an idea forming in my mind. There were six iron gray rocks, jutting out of the sea. I had noticed them the day we had searched the island. And of course, rocks like that have a name. Long and slender with pointed tops, standing upright in the water . . .

They're called needles.

I'm not exactly sure what happened next but I do know that it all happened at the same time.

There was a soft explosion, just where Tim was standing. The earth underneath his feet seemed to separate, falling away.

Tim screamed and his arm jerked. The butter knife spun in the air, the sun glinting off the blade.

I yelled out and threw myself forward. Somehow my hands managed to grab hold of Tim's shirt.

"Don't kill me!" Tim whimpered.

"I'm not killing you, you idiot!" I yelled. "I'm saving you!"

We rolled back together, away from the edge of the cliff . . . an edge that was now several inches closer to us than it had been seconds before. I was dazed and there was grass in my mouth, but I realized that the killer had struck again. There had been a small explosive charge buried in the ground at the end of the cliff. Someone had detonated it, and if I hadn't managed to grab hold of Tim, he would have fallen down toward the sea, only to crash onto the needles two hundred feet below.

We lay on the grass, panting. The sun was beating down on us. It was difficult to see. But then I became aware of a shadow moving toward us. I rolled over and looked up at the figure, limping toward us, a radio transmitter in one hand and a gun in the other.

"Well, well, well," he said. "It looks as if my little plan has finally come unstuck. And just when everything was going so well, too!"

Tim stared at the man. At his single eye, his single leg, his huge beard. "It's . . . it's . . ." he began.

"It's Horatio Randle," I said. "Captain of the *Silver Medal*, the boat that brought us here."

"You got it in one, young lad!" he said.

"But that's not his real name," I went on. "Randle is an anagram. If you switch around the letters, you get—"

"Endral!" Tim exclaimed.

"Nadler," I said. "I think this must be Johnny Nadler. Your old school friend from St. Egbert's."

The captain put down the radio transmitter. He had used it, of course, to set off the explosive charge a few moments before. He didn't let go of the gun. With his free hand, he reached up and pulled off the fake beard, the wig, and the eye patch. At the same time, he twisted around and released the leg that he'd had tied up behind his back. It took only a few seconds but at once I recognized the thin-faced teenager I had seen in the photograph.

"It seems you've worked it all out," he muttered. His accent had changed, too. He was no longer the jolly captain. He was a killer. And he was mad.

"Yes," I said.

"But it's impossible!" Tim burbled. "He couldn't have killed all the others. We looked! There was nobody else on the island!"

"It was Nadler all along," I said. I glanced at him. The wind raced past and the waves crashed down.

He smiled. "Do go on," he snarled.

"I know what you did," I said. "Last Wednesday, you met us all at the dock, disguised as a captain. You'd sent everyone invitations to this reunion on the island and you even offered to pay a thousand dollars to make sure that they'd all come. Rory McDougal had nothing to do with it, of course. You'd killed him before we even set sail."

"That's right," Nadler said. He was smiling now. There was something horrible about that smile. He was sure this was one story I wouldn't be telling anyone else.

"You killed Rory and you left the poisoned chocolate for Sylvie. Then you dropped us on the island and sailed away again. There was no need for you to stay. Everything was already prepared."

"Are you saying . . . he wasn't here when he killed everyone?" Tim asked. He was still lying on the grass. There was a buttercup lodged behind his ear.

"That's right. Don't you remember what Mark told us when we were looking at the picture? He said that Johnny Nadler wanted to be an inventor when he left school. He said he was always playing with planes and cars." I glanced at the transmitter lying on the ground just a few feet away. "I assume they were radio-controlled planes and cars," I said.

"That's right!" Tim said. "He was brilliant, Nick! He once landed a helicopter on the science teacher's head!"

"Well, that's how he killed everyone on the island—after

he'd finished with Rory McDougal and Sylvie Binns." I took a deep breath, wondering if there was anything I could do. Tim was right next to the edge of the cliff. I was a couple of feet in front of him. We were both lying down. Nadler was standing over us, aiming with the gun. If we so much as moved, he could shoot us both. I had to keep talking and hope that I might somehow find a way to distract him.

"Janet Rhodes was stabbed with an Eiffel Tower," I went on. "But I noticed that there was a tear in the canopy above her bed. I should have put two and two together and realized that the Eiffel Tower was always there, above the bed. It must have been mounted on some sort of spring mechanism. Nadler knew that was where she'd be sleeping. All he had to do was press a button and send the model plunging down. He was probably miles away when he killed her."

"That's right!" Nadler giggled. "I was back on the mainland. I was nowhere near!"

"But what about the face you saw?" Tim asked. "The skull at the window! Brenda saw it, too!"

"You've already answered that one, Tim," I said. "A remote-control helicopter or something with a mask hanging underneath. Nadler controlled that, too. It was easy!"

"But how could he see us?"

I glanced at Nadler and he nodded. He was happy for me to explain how it had been done.

"The whole island is covered in cameras," I said. "That

was Rory's security system. We've been watched from the moment we arrived. Nadler knew where we were every minute of the day."

"Right again!" Nadler grinned. He was pleased with himself, I could see that. "It was easy to hack into McDougal's security system and redirect the pictures to my own TV monitor. I was even able to watch you in the bath!"

"That's outrageous!" Tim was blushing. He knew that Nadler would have seen him playing with his plastic duck.

"Nadler had positioned the globe up on the roof," I went on. "If we'd gone up and looked we'd probably have found some sort of ramp with a simple switch. He waited until Libby Goldman came out of the front door and then he pressed the button that released the globe. It rolled forward and that was that. She never had a chance. He killed Eric and Brenda the same way. First he turned out the lights. Then he fired a bullet and brought down an organ pipe . . . both by remote control." I paused. "How about Mark Tyler?" I asked.

"The javelin was hidden in the branches of a tree," Nadler explained. "It was on a giant rubber band. Remote control again. It was just like a crossbow." He giggled for a second time. "Only bigger."

Well that explained the leaves. Some of them must have traveled with the javelin when it was fired.

"And that just left you, Tim," I said. "Nadler had to wait until you came out here. Then he was going to blow the ground out from beneath your feet and watch you fall onto the needles below. And with you dead, his revenge would be complete."

"Revenge?" Tim was genuinely puzzled. "But why did he want revenge? We never did anything to him!"

"I think it was because he came in second," I said. I turned to Nadler. "You came in second in every subject at school. And the boat you picked us up in. It was called the *Silver Medal*. I guess you chose the name on purpose. Because that's what you're given when you come in second."

"That's right." Nadler nodded and now his face had darkened and his lips were twisted into an expression of pain. His finger tightened on the trigger and he looked at me with hatred in his eyes. "I came in second in math, second in chemistry, second in French, second in geography, second in history, second in music, and second in sports. I even came in second in needlework, even though my embroidered tea towel was much more beautiful than your brother's stupid handkerchief!"

"It was a lovely handkerchief!" Tim said.

"Shut up!" Nadler screamed, and for a moment I was afraid he was going to shoot Tim then and there. "Do you have any idea how horrible it is coming in second?" he went on. Saliva flecked at his lips. The hand with the gun never moved. "Coming in last doesn't matter. Coming in fifth or sixth . . . who cares? But when you come in second, everyone knows. You've just missed! You've missed getting the prize by just a few points. And everyone feels sorry for you. Poor old Johnny! He couldn't quite make it. He wasn't quite good enough."

He took a deep breath. "I've been coming in second all my life. I go for jobs and I get down to the last two in the interviews but it's always the other person who gets it. I went out with a girl but then she decided to marry someone else because as far as she was concerned, I was Number Two. When I've tried to sell my inventions, I've discovered that someone else has always gotten there first. Number Two! Number Two! Number Two! I hate being Number Two . . . !

"And it's all your fault!" He pointed the gun at Tim and now the fury was back in his eyes. "It all started at St. Egbert's! That hateful school! That was where I started coming in second and that was why I decided to have my revenge. You all thought you were clever beating me at everything. Well, I've shown you! I've killed the whole lot of you and I've done it in exactly the way you deserve!"

"You haven't killed me!" Tim exclaimed.

I didn't think it was a good idea to point this out. Nadler steadied the gun. "I'm going to do that now," he said. "Your body will still end up smashing into the needles, so everything will have worked out the way it was meant to." He nodded at me. "I'll have to kill you, too, of course," he continued. "You weren't meant to be here, but I don't mind. You sound too clever for your own good. I'm going to enjoy killing you, too!"

He took aim.

"No!" I shouted.

He fired at Tim.

"Missed!" Tim laughed and rolled to one side. He was still laughing when he rolled over the side of the cliff.

"Tim!" I yelled.

"Now it's your turn," Nadler said.

I closed my eyes. There was nothing I could do.

There was a long pause. I opened them again.

Nadler was still standing, but even as I watched he crumpled to the ground. Eric Draper, the fat solicitor, was standing behind him. There was blood all over his shirt and he was deathly pale. But he was still alive. He was holding the blunderbuss, which he must have taken from the bear. He hadn't fired it. He had used it like a club and knocked Nadler out.

"He only wounded me . . ." he gasped. "I woke up this morning. I came to find you . . ."

But I wasn't interested in Eric Draper, even if he had just saved my life. I crawled over to the cliff edge and looked down, expecting to see Tim, smashed to pieces, on the rocks below.

"Hello, Nick!" Tim said.

There was a bush growing out of the side of the cliff. He had fallen right onto it. I held out a hand. Tim took it. I pulled him to safety and we both lay there in the sun, exhausted, glad to be alive.

We found the *Silver Medal* moored at the jetty and I steered it back toward the mainland. Eric was slumped on the deck. Johnny Nadler was down below, tied up with so much rope that only his head was showing. We weren't taking any chances after what had happened. We had already radioed ahead to the police. They would be waiting when we got to the mainland. Tim was standing next to me. We had left six dead bodies behind us on Crocodile Island. Well, I warned you that it was going to be a horror story.

"I'm sorry I thought you were the killer," Tim said. He was looking even more sheepish than . . . well, a sheep.

"It's all right, Tim," I said. "It's a mistake anyone could have made." He swayed on his feet and suddenly I felt sorry for him. "Do you want to sit down?" I asked. "It's going to take us a while to get back."

Tim shook his head. "No." He blushed. "I can't!"

"Why not?"

"That bush I fell into. It was very prickly. My bottom's full of . . ."

"What?"

". . . needles!"

I pushed down on the throttle and the boat surged forward. Behind us, Crocodile Island shimmered in the morning mist until at last it had disappeared.

Turn the page for a preview of

SOUTH BY SOUTHEAST

a Diamond Brothers Mystery

MCGUFFIN

What can I tell you about Camden Town? It's a place in north London with a market and a canal. What you can't find in the market you'll find floating in the canal—only cheaper.

And that's why we'd moved to Camden Town. Because it was cheap. Our new offices were small and sleazy but that was okay because so were most of our clients. We hadn't taken much with us. Just some old furniture and some bad memories. And the door. It was cheaper to bring the door with us than get another one painted.

TIM DIAMOND INC.
PRIVATE DETECTIVE

That's what it said on the glass.

They were the last words Jake McGuffin ever read. But when you're being chased by two Dutch killers with a knife and a gun and your name on both of them, you don't have time to start a paperback book.

It was a long, hot summer. Although I didn't know it then, it was going to be longer and hotter for me than for anyone else. The day it all started, it was my turn to make lunch—but I'd just discovered there was no lunch left to make. I'd done my best. I'd gotten a tray ready with plates, knives, forks, napkins, and even a flower I'd found growing on the bathroom wall. All that was missing was the food.

"Is that it?" Tim asked as I carried it in. He was sitting behind his desk, making paper boats out of pages from the phone book. "A carton of milk?"

"Half a carton," I replied. "We had the other half for breakfast." It was true. Half a carton of long-life milk was all that stood between us and starvation. "I'll get some glasses," I said.

"Don't bother." Tim reached for a cardboard box on the corner of his desk. He turned it upside down. A single straw fell out. "That's the last straw," he announced.

I'd been living with my big brother, Herbert Timothy Simple, ever since my parents decided to emigrate to Australia. Herbert called himself Tim Diamond. He also called himself a private detective. Neither was true. He wouldn't have been able to find a fingerprint on the end of his own finger. Dead bodies made him feel queasy. When it came to pursuing an investigation, he was so hopeless that the investigation usually ended up pursuing him.

I gazed sadly at the milk. "You need a job, Tim," I said.

"I've applied for jobs, Nick," Tim protested. He slid open a drawer in his desk. It was bulging with letters. "Look! I've applied for hundreds of jobs."

"How many rejections have you had?" I asked.

He scowled. "These *are* the rejections." He fumbled in the pile for a minute and pulled one out, his face brightening. "Here's one I haven't heard from yet," he said.

"Maybe your application got lost in the mail."

Tim opened the letter and spread it out in front of him. "Head of security at the Canadian Bank in Pall Mall," he read out. "Forty thousand dollars a year plus lunch vouchers and car. In other words, meals and wheels."

"When will you hear?" I asked.

"Don't worry. The phone'll ring . . ."

"We don't have a phone," I reminded him. "We got cut off."

Tim's face fell. He folded the letter and put it back in the drawer.

"Things aren't so bad," he muttered. "I'll get a case sooner or later. I bet you any day now somebody's going to knock on the door."

Somebody knocked on the door.

Tim gulped like he'd just swallowed a chicken bone. He looked around him. What with the lunch tray on the desk, the paper boats, and everything else, the office hardly looked like the headquarters of a successful private eye. And here was a potential client knocking at the door! For a moment he froze. Then we both went into action.

The paper boats went into the bin. Tim opened another

drawer and threw the knives, forks, and napkins inside. At the same time, I grabbed the milk carton and slipped it into a vase on a shelf. That just left the tray. Tim handed it to me. I looked for somewhere, to put it. I couldn't see anywhere so I put it on a chair and sat on it.

"Come in!" Tim called out. He was bent over the desk, scribbling away at a blank sheet of paper. It would have looked more impressive if he'd been using the right end of the pen.

The door opened.

Our visitor was carrying a gun—and it was the gun that I looked at first. It was small, snub-nosed, a dull, metallic gray. So was the visitor. He was only a little taller than me and he was so pale he could have just stepped out of one of those old black-and-white films they show on TV. He had a square chin, close-cropped hair, and small eyes that seemed to be hiding behind the thick lenses of his glasses. Either he was extremely shortsighted or his optician was. Or maybe it was just that he felt safer behind bulletproof glasses.

He shut the door behind him. It must have been raining outside because there were big drops clinging to his forehead and dripping off the hem of his coat. Or maybe he was sweating. "You Tim Diamond?" he asked.

"Yeah, I'm Tim Diamond," Tim agreed.

The man moved farther into the room and saw me. For a moment the gun pointed my way and my hands flickered automatically toward a position somewhere above my head. "Who are you?" he demanded.

"I'm Nick Diamond," I said. "His brother."

His eyes traveled down. "Why are you sitting on a tray?" he demanded.

"Because I feel like a cup of tea." It was the first thing to come into my head but the answer must have satisfied him because a moment later, walking over to the window, he'd forgotten me.

"I didn't catch your name," Tim said.

"Jake McGuffin." The man peered out of the window, his eyes as narrow as the venetian blind we'd sold the week before. He glanced back over his shoulder at the door. "Is that the only way in?"

Tim nodded. "Are you in some sort of trouble?" he asked.

"Somebody's trying to kill me," McGuffin said.

He turned away from the window just as a high-velocity bullet fired from the street drilled a neat hole through the pane, flashed across the room a bare inch from his face, smashed the vase on the shelf opposite, and exposed the carton of milk I had hidden there earlier. Milk fountained out.

"What makes you think that, Mr. McStuffing?" Tim inquired.

I was staggered. Even McGuffin had gone pale. But

evidently Tim just hadn't noticed there was anything wrong. The truth was he was so wrapped up in his own performance that he probably wouldn't have noticed if his visitor had been hit then and there. I edged closer to the filing cabinet, ready to hurl myself behind it if any more bullets blasted into the room.

McGuffin slipped the gun into a shoulder holster and moved across the carpet, keeping clear of the window. "I need to use a phone," he said. The words came out fast, urgent.

"Why?" Tim asked.

McGuffin hesitated. I think he still hadn't figured Tim out. But then he had other things on his mind.

"You can tell me, Mr. McMuffin," Tim went on. He tapped his nose. "I'm a private nose with an eye for trouble. Trouble is my middle name."

McGuffin looked around the room. If he could have seen a telephone I reckon he would have used the cord to strangle Tim and then made his call uninterrupted. But whoever was waiting for him outside had him cornered. Time was running out. He had no choice. "Okay," he said. "I'll tell you."

He sat down opposite Tim and took out a cigarette. "You got a light?" he asked.

Tim switched on his desk light. McGuffin scrunched his cigarette on the desktop. He seemed to have gotten a lot older in the last few minutes. "Listen," he said. "I'm an agent. It doesn't matter who I work for."

"Who do you work for?" Tim asked.

"It doesn't matter. I'm on the track of a man called Charon. He's a killer, an assassin, the head of a murder organization that's bigger than General Motors."

Tim was puzzled. "Charon?" he asked. "What sort of name is that?"

"It's a code name," McGuffin explained. "It comes out of the Greek myths. You ever hear of Hades, the Greek underworld? In the old legends, it's where people went when they died. Charon was the person who took them there. He was the ferryman of the dead."

The sun must have gone behind a cloud. For the first time that summer I felt cold. Maybe it was the breeze coming in through the bullet hole.

"Nobody knows who Charon really is," McGuffin went on. "He can disguise himself at the drop of a hat. They say he's got so many faces his own mother wouldn't recognize him."

"Do you know his mother?" Tim asked.

"No." McGuffin took a deep breath. "There's only one way to recognize Charon," he said. "He's lost a finger."

"Whose finger?" Tim asked.

"His own. He only has nine fingers."

Tim smiled. "So that'll help you finger him!"

McGuffin closed his eyes for a few seconds. He must have hoped he was dreaming and that when he opened them he'd be somewhere else. "Right," he said at last. "But I've got no time. Charon is about to kill a Russian diplomat called Boris Kusenov."

"I've heard of him," I muttered. And it was true. I'd seen the name in the last newspaper I'd read. It had been underneath my chips.

"If Kusenov dies, that's it," McGuffin went on. "The Iron Curtain goes back up. There'll be another arms race. Maybe even war . . ."

"As bad as that?" Tim asked.

"I'm the only man who can stop him. I know when Charon plans to kill him. And I know how. I've got to make that call."

Tim shrugged. "That's too bad, McNothing. We don't have a phone."

"No phone . . ." For a moment I thought he was going to murder Tim. He'd told us everything. And he'd gotten nothing for it. His hands writhed briefly. Maybe he was imagining them around Tim's throat.

"There's a phone booth around the corner, in Skin Lane," I suggested.

McGuffin had forgotten I was even in the room. He looked at me, then at the bullet hole. The bullet hole was like a single eye and that seemed to be looking at me, too. "It's an alley," I added.

"Outside." McGuffin licked his lips. I could see his problem. If he waited here much longer, Charon would come in and get him. And next time it might not be a single bullet.

One grenade and we'd all be permanently disconnected, like the telephone. On the other hand, if he stepped out into the street he'd be a walking target. And I doubted if Charon would miss a second time.

But McGuffin was obviously used to thinking on his feet. Suddenly he was out of the chair and over on the other side of the room, where Tim's raincoat was hanging on a hook. "I'll give you fifty bucks for the coat," McGuffin said.

"But you've already got a coat," Tim observed.

"I've got to get out of here without being seen."

McGuffin pulled off his own coat. Underneath he was wearing an off-white suit that had probably been white when he put it on. It didn't quite hide the gun, jutting out of a shoulder holster where most people carry a wallet. He put on the raincoat, folding the collar up so that it hid most of his face. Finally he produced fifty dollars out of nowhere and threw them down on the desk, five ten-dollar bills that were the best thing I'd seen all day. Tim wasn't going to complain either. The coat had only cost him ten dollars in the second-hand shop, and even they had probably made enough profit out of it to buy a third hand.

McGuffin took a deep breath. He hesitated for one last moment. And then he was gone. The door clicked shut behind him.

I got off the tray. "What do you think?" I asked.

Tim opened his eyes. The money was sitting right in front of him. "Fifty smackers!" he exclaimed.

"I wonder who he was working for?"

"Forget it, Nick," Tim pocketed the money. "It's none of our business. I'm just glad we're not involved."

I picked up McGuffin's coat, meaning to hang it back on the hook. As I lifted it, something fell out of one of the pockets. It was a key. There was a plastic tag attached to it and in bright red letters: *Room 605, London International Hotel.*

I looked at the key. Tim looked at me. We were involved all right.